"CASH? JAKE?" I stepped around the massive kitchen table, piled high with electronics, and out into the sunshine. Blinded for a moment by the brightness, I didn't immediately notice the person in the pool.

When I did, I also registered that he was facedown.

Oh, no. Not good.

Caro Lamont, amateur sleuth and well-respected animal therapist to Laguna Beach's pampered pets, works with office mate and tech wizard, Graham Cash, whose beloved Scottish Fold tabby cat, Toria, is purported to have anger management issues. But when Caro drops by the charming Brit's Tudor-inspired mansion to return Toria, she finds his business partner dead and Cash missing.

Caro is left with the cuddly cat and a lot of unanswered questions. Is Cash the killer, or has he been kidnapped? What's up with the angry next door neighbor? And what about Cash's girlfriend, Heidi, who isn't sharing everything she knows with homicide detective Judd Malone?

Suddenly there are more secrets and intrigues than there are titles in England.

Betty, hiding in restaurant shrubbery, and wannabe investigative reporter Callum MacAvoy, who seems to be constantly underfoot, and you've got a cat and mouse mystery of the first order.

Caro's got to solve this murder before the killer lets the cat out of the bag.

The Pampered Pets Mysteries from Bell Bridge Books

Desperate Housedogs

Get Fluffy

Kitty Kitty Bang Bang

Yip/Tuck

Fifty Shades of Greyhound

The Girl with the Dachshund Tattoo

Downton Tabby

Raiders of the Lost Bark (coming soon!)

Downton Tabby

by

Sparkle Abbey

Bell Bridge Books

Bell Bridge Books
PO BOX 300921
Memphis, TN 38130
Print ISBN: 978-1-61194-624-6

Bell Bridge Books is an Imprint of BelleBooks, Inc.

We at BelleBooks enjoy hearing from readers.
Visit our websites
BelleBooks.com
BellBridgeBooks.com
ImaJinnBooks.com

10 9 8 7 6 5 4 3 2 1

Cover design: Debra Dixon
Interior design: Hank Smith
Photo/Art credits:
Illustration (manipulated) © sababaJJ | iStockphoto.com
Face (manipulated) © Subarashii21 | Dreamstime.com
Collar © Roughcollie | Dreamstime.com
Paw Print © Booka1 | Dreamstime.com
magnifying glass © Yudesign | Dreamstime.com

:Ltdc:01:

Dedication

This book is dedicated to family. Ours and yours. To cousins, aunts, uncles, brothers, sisters, in-laws, outlaws, and friends who have become family. The love of a family, whether by birth or by choice, is a blessing.

Chapter One

THE IRISH SETTER and I had a lot in common, and I don't just mean hair color.

Cork was a former show dog. I was a former Texas beauty queen. We were both named after places, and we both had families with issues.

My family drama would have to wait, but I thought I could assist with hers.

"So, Carolina, what do you think? Is my girl depressed?" Spencer Hogsworth, Cork's owner, bounded into the room. He ran a hand down the dog's feathery chestnut fur and gave her a pat on the head before continuing around us to fling open the drapes.

"I want your expert opinion," he continued. "You came highly recommended, by none other than Hollywood's darling, Diana Knight, as Laguna Beach's top pet therapist."

He said "top" with such emphasis you'd think I performed life-saving heart surgery, instead of sanity-saving dog and cat therapy.

I'd had to start the day without coffee, which isn't a good thing for me, or for the people who are unfortunate enough to have to interact with me sans caffeine, but I was trying very hard to be patient. And Spencer Hogsworth, bless his heart, was certainly trying my patience.

He'd bounced in and out of the room like a terrier with a tennis ball while I was trying to evaluate his dog, creating a distraction that made it difficult to assess her current state.

Cork was five, and the previous season had been her last year on the show circuit. I suspected she was more than ready to retire. I'd rebelled at a much younger age (in people years anyway), walking out on the Miss Texas pageant at eighteen, much to my mother's chagrin.

"I don't believe Cork is depressed." I slid down on the floor next to the beautiful dog and ran my fingers along her back. She flipped her head, ears flopping, and nudged my hand so I'd be sure to reach a spot on the back of her neck.

"What then?" Spencer folded his tall, lanky frame into a puffy, lime-green chair. "What are we to do? Just look at the havoc Cork is causing." He gestured toward the lavish post-modern living room.

"Havoc" was a bit strong, but Cork did have a problem with sitting still, and lately, according to Spencer, she'd been getting into everything she could. Recently, her inquisitiveness had turned destructive and she'd apparently chewed up Spencer's brand-new six-hundred-dollar Armani wallet. And all of his credit cards.

"A simple solution we can try . . . ," I paused, waiting for Spencer to give me his full attention. He stared off into space, lost in a reverie, perhaps thinking about all the competitions represented by the shiny trophies lined up like soldiers on the floor-to-ceiling glass shelves covering the far wall. Each one must surely represent a memory.

I was tempted to snap my fingers, like I often did with the dogs, but I resisted. "Spencer?"

"Yes?" He shifted in the chair to look at me.

"A very easy thing to start with is exercise." I gave Cork one more belly rub and then brushed the dog hair from my jeans and stood. She scrambled to her feet. "Irish Setters need at least an hour of exercise a day. I know that's not news to you." I held up my hand to stop him from interrupting. "And I'm sure you exercise Cork, but my guess is you both have a less active lifestyle now that you're not constantly training for dog shows."

"True." Spencer popped out of the chair and began straightening the pillows on the massive ultra-modern couch. "That seems too easy."

"Let's try it." I was sure both Spencer and Cork were going to need a new interest to focus on now that their show days were over. But getting Cork more exercise would be a beginning. "I'll check back in a week and we'll re-evaluate how y'all are doing. Does that sound okay?"

"Yes, yes, we can try it." Spencer crossed to pull open the room's French doors and let Cork outside.

I smiled as the rollicking redhead raced across the length of the backyard and back, and then pounced on a leaf. "I'd like to see her get at least thirty minutes of exercise, twice a day. The dog park would be great, weather permitting, because there she would really have room to let loose and run."

Spencer agreed to the increased exercise and trips to the dog park. I left my phone number with him and encouraged him to call if he had any questions or if anything new came up with Cork.

Once outside, I stood on the front steps a moment and inhaled the crisp sea air. I'd like some room to run myself but I had a busy day ahead, so I didn't think time for letting loose was in the cards for me.

When I'd arrived, I'd left the top down on my silver vintage Mercedes roadster, and the morning sun had warmed the leather. I tossed my bag in the back, slid behind the wheel, and reviewed the day so far.

It had been a bumpy morning.

Let me catch y'all up.

IT HAD STARTED with my need for morning caffeine. I'd filled the pot with water, scooped in my favorite organic grind, pushed the button, and waited for the aroma of fresh brewed coffee.

I waited. And waited.

Nada. Nothing.

My coffeepot had up and died. I know, minor stuff, right? Fair enough. I'd just stop at the Koffee Klatch on my way to the office and then pick up a new coffeepot after work. They make great coffee, the place is not out of my way, and I'd planned the morning to catch up on paperwork, so no biggie.

About that paperwork. I despise it. Now that might sound kind of strong, but I really do. Here's the deal, I'm a pet therapist. I work with problem pets, and so I think it goes without saying that paperwork isn't my favorite part of the gig. The pets are. What could be better than a day spent with people and their fur babies?

Laguna Beach is a great place to be in the pet business because there are more registered pets in the community than there are children. Needless to say, folks here are crazy about their furry family members. I can relate; I'm crazy about mine, too.

Back in Texas, I was trained as a people therapist, but, thanks to my lying, cheating, ex-husband and a major scandal courtesy of the aforementioned ex, I'd lost my license to practice and had decided to leave my beloved Lone Star State and start over. Which leads me to the next pothole in this morning that had already been headed downhill faster than a runaway wagon.

I had showered and dressed (jeans and a new Akris white cotton crepe tunic I'd paid way too much for) and taken my pooch, Dogbert, for a quick walk around the block.

Back at home, Thelma and Louise, the two felines in charge of the household, checked to make sure I'd left them sufficient provisions for their day and then went back to soaking up the sun.

I reached down to pet the two and glanced outside. My patio doors framed a view I never took for granted. Blue sky touched bluer water that danced along the coast and reached out toward tomorrow.

Prodding myself to stop daydreaming and get moving, I turned from the picture-postcard view. My home, unlike the *House Beautiful* home I'd grown up in, was best described as "lived-in chic." Or at least that's how I saw it. Bookshelves jammed with books, not for display, but actually read and loved. Comfortable people and pet-friendly furniture, sturdy furnishings accessorized with eclectic bric-a-brac, the remnants of a dog-treat recipe experiment from the night before. My home.

I grabbed a few of the new dog biscuits and threw them into my Coach tote, snagged my phone from the dining-room table, and had been fixin' to head out to meet with Spencer and Cork.

Just as I'd been about to toss my phone in my bag, it rang.

"Hello," I'd answered as I picked up my car keys.

"Don't hang up." Well, shoot. It was Geoffrey, my ex.

Don't hang up? Hells bells, I hadn't heard from him in over a year, and I wouldn't have even answered if I'd known it was him.

"What do you want?" I snapped.

Y'all are probably thinking that was a bit rude of me, and it's true. My mama had raised me better and would have been absolutely appalled at my bad manners. But you see, I've come a long way in the not-pretending department. And though I'm usually very polite, I'm frankly not sure of the proper greeting for a yellow-bellied, lying cheat whom you once loved. A man who slept with a client, broke your heart, and destroyed your life. At least my life had sure seemed destroyed at the time.

"Carolina, it's so nice to hear your voice. Did I catch you at a bad time?" The louse must want something. I would bet good money Geoff wasn't simply calling me to shoot the breeze.

"I was about to walk out the door," I told him.

"Where to?" His voice was as smooth as Kentucky bourbon, just like I remembered. The slightest flavor of the south in those cultured tones, but where it had once thrilled me, it now grated on my nerves.

"Work." I continued collecting my things.

"That's right, you counsel canines and kitties." He laughed.

I did not.

"Get to the point, Geoffrey." I'd been patient, but I was done talking, and my short fuse had nothing to do with my red hair and everything to do with my Texas baloney detector. And if I'm honest, maybe just a little, my lack of caffeine.

"Sorry to hold you up." I pictured his face in my mind and had a momentary flash of wondering if he'd changed physically. I hadn't seen him since the last court date. "Here's the thing, Carolina. I'm going to be in LA on business, and I'd like to see you."

"Why?" The question shot right out of me.

"Why not?" His response had been just as quick. "I think we both need some closure."

"No thanks, Geoffrey." I got in my car. "I've got closure."

And with that I pushed the disconnect button.

SO, AFTER THAT rocky start, I have to say I believe I'd done a pretty dang good job of focusing on Spencer and Cork and maintaining my cool.

But now I was ready for some coffee. Beyond ready. I started the car and put it in gear.

Koffee Klatch, here I come.

The Koffee Klatch was a local coffeehouse right on Pacific Coast Highway and on my way to the office. There was no good reason for it this time of day, but the line was endless. Verdi, our part-time reception-ist at the office, also worked at the local coffeehouse. She was behind the wide wooden counter this morning, but even her speed and efficiency couldn't move people through fast enough. Granted, my caffeine defi-ciency may have impacted my view of the line.

My impatience must have shown on my face because the lovely, multi-pierced, burgundy-haired Verdi didn't attempt to chat. She just handed me my usual hazelnut latte and took my money. I'd always known she was one sharp chick, and her silent competence confirmed it. I thanked her and left. Caffeine in hand. Finally.

The aroma soothed me as I took a satisfying sip. She'd given me a large. Like I said, the girl was sharp.

When I arrived at the office, the building was locked up tight. As you've probably already figured out, if Verdi was on duty at the Koffee Klatch, she was not on duty at the office. I share office space with a realtor, a psychic, and an investment advisor. None of us have a ton of administrative needs, so it works out.

A delivery van was pulled up out front, and the driver had parked himself at our door. His I've-got-other-places-to-be posture said he wasn't happy with not being able to drop his delivery and run.

"Here ya go." He thrust a package at me. "Sign here."

I shifted my bag and my latte and took it. It was a big envelope and a bit awkward to hold. And undoubtedly not for me. Suzanne, the psychic, got documents occasionally. Or it could be some official papers for Kay, the realtor. I glanced at the envelope which was addressed to 2Gyz with a return address of SIS Tech and an address in the UK. Oh, right. I'd momentarily forgotten about our new officemates, a couple of twenty-something techies who'd leased the vacant space. My brain clearly needed more caffeine.

I signed where the man in shorts indicated. He was already poised for the sprint back to his truck. I unlocked the door and flipped on the office lights then dropped the package on the reception desk.

I turned away and slammed into a bulky wall of a man who somehow had managed to come through the front door without my hearing him. Maybe we needed one of those bells that dings when someone comes in.

"Who are you?" I took a step back ready to defend myself if necessary. My best friend, Diana, and I had taken a self-defense class, a Valentine's Day gift from Sam Gallanos, the man in my life. I felt like his choice of a gift was a pointed comment on the life I lead. Anyway, we'd learned a lot in class, and, even as big as this guy was, I knew I could take him.

"I'm so sorry, ma'am." He also backed up. "I did not mean to scare you."

"What do you want?" I was on a roll. Again, yes, I know it wasn't a polite response and my mama would be appalled and all that, but in my defense I was a bit startled. And my mental tank was still low on caffeine.

"Sorry." The man took another step back. "I had some car trouble out front, and I wondered if I could borrow your phone to call my auto club. Cell phone's dead."

Well, nothing nefarious about that. And to be perfectly honest, now that I'd gotten a good look at the guy, he sure as heck didn't look like a mugger. Wrinkled khakis and a dark-blue shirt. Sandy-haired, broad-faced, and with a bit of a paunch. Maybe I'd overreacted. Just a little.

"The phone is right here." I reached over the wide reception desk and placed the phone on the counter. "Go ahead and make your call."

"Thank you so much, ma'am." He held out a beefy hand. "I sure appreciate it."

I shook his bear-sized paw.

"Are you the accountant, the psychic, or with the computer guys?"

He noted the sign at the front door which detailed the businesses located in the building.

"I'm actually the pet therapist." I pointed at the PAWS info.

"A pet therapist? I used to have a dog. Charlie. I loved that dog." He smiled the wistful smile of all of us who've lost a pet.

Now I felt even worse that I'd been so rude.

I left him at the reception desk to make his phone call and unlocked the door to my office. I couldn't hear his conversation, but he must have been successful in contacting his auto club because he poked his head around the corner and thanked me again.

"You're welcome." I smiled at him, feeling a little bad I'd immediately thought the worst.

"I'll just wait out by my car. They said they'd been here in ten minutes."

"Okay, I hope the rest of your day goes better."

See, I guess my morning wasn't so bad in comparison. I hadn't had car trouble. Only coffee trouble. It's all about perspective isn't it?

Ah, yes, perspective.

I settled in and got down to work transferring my notes to the client files on my computer. To be honest, my concentration wasn't worth two cents. The phone call from my ex nagged at me. I didn't want Geoffrey in California. I didn't want Geoffrey in my head, but there he was. Enough so that I kept having to reread the same sentence as I worked to update the files I needed to take care of before my afternoon appointments.

"Hello? Is anyone about?"

"In here." I glanced up from my paperwork.

It was Cash, one of the partners in the tech company I mentioned earlier. His name was actually Graham Cash, but everyone calls him "Cash." He was constantly rumpled, baby-faced handsome, and charmingly British.

The other partner was Jake, a blond surfer type and California native. I wasn't sure how they'd met but the two had made millions, possibly billions, with a series of mobile apps. You know, those little programs that work on your phone. They'd been in the right place at the right time and had been riding that wave ever since. Or as my Grandma Tillie would've said, they'd been "ridin' a gravy train with biscuit wheels." In the part of Texas I'm from we're more versed in gravy than surf.

Today Cash sported his typical billionaire-geek office attire: jeans, an expensive but wrinkled dress shirt, and a weathered, brown leather bomber jacket. Toria, his adorable Scottish Fold cat, was tucked under his arm.

"Morning, Caro. Toria's going to help me out today. Aren't you, luv?" He scratched the cat under the chin, and she rubbed her face against his.

Toria often accompanied the tech tycoon. A sturdy feline, as was common in the breed, the grey silky tabby was a little, um, more sturdy than most. I suspected a bit of spoiling.

Cash strolled in and plopped down in the chair by my desk. I reached over to give Toria a proper greeting. "Good morning, girlfriend, and how are you today?" She leaned into my hand in answer.

"You checked her over, right?" He scratched the cat's soft, wide head. "No signs of problems."

"Nothing." A week ago, Cash had asked me to examine Toria for any signs of behavioral problems. Apparently, someone had reported she'd been aggressive, which not only did I find hard to believe but would also be highly unusual in the breed. "I'd recommend you have Dr. Darling give her a once-over to make sure she's not having any health issues, but behavior-wise I didn't find a thing."

"See? No problem, m'lady." He lifted her to eye level and looked into her green saucer-like eyes. "Falsely accused. I knew you were too well-mannered to misbehave like that."

"Maybe she's simply bored." I smiled at the flicker of shock in his intelligent blue eyes. "Sometimes a normally passive cat will become a little forceful in their play if they have a lot of pent-up energy."

"But what is one to do?" He stroked the cat's back. "I should think you can't take a cat for a proper walk."

"Perhaps you and Jake can develop an app to entertain Toria."

He stared off into space, apparently lost in the possibilities.

I waved a hand in front of his face. "Cash, I was kidding."

"You have a cat, don't you?" He continued to absently stroke Toria's fur. "So we'd have some built-in beta testers."

"I have two cats, Thelma and Louise." I laughed. "Common house cats, though, not pure-bred royalty like Toria."

"Old girl thinks she's an aristo-cat anyway." A wide grin creased his cheeks. "And a royal name to boot. After Queen Victoria."

Cash stood, ignoring the cat fur that now covered his dark blue jeans. "An early patron of animal rights. One of the few for her time. She's the royal who authorized adding that important prefix to our Royal

Society for the Prevention of Cruelty to Animals."

"Interesting stuff." I looked up at the two. "In fact, I can't believe I didn't know that."

"See, I'm more than just another pretty face." His bright-blue eyes twinkled. And then cradling Toria against him, he turned to go.

"Oh, Cash, by the way there's a package for you on the front desk."

"Thanks." He disappeared into the reception area. "Come on, Toria. I'm positive at this point we've got hundreds of bloody emails to answer."

An hour flew by as I updated files, organized notes, and made my list for the day. Yep, I'm one of those. Don't judge. I love my daily list. I know it's about control, but I don't care. It's a little coping thing, and it works for me.

I could hear Cash in the office next door. His music was some sort of Celtic instrumental. Usually he used headphones, but today he'd apparently opted for speakers. Didn't bother me at all. It was lilting and relaxing. I'd made good progress on my paperwork.

"Caro, could Toria hang with you for a bit?"

I looked up from my computer. Cash was suddenly back at my door, and I realized the music had stopped.

"Jake just rang me and I've got to pop by the house for a few minutes. Twenty to thirty minutes tops."

"Sure." I took Toria from him. I had at least another thirty minutes of file updating work to do.

"Be back in a jiffy," Cash called over his shoulder.

I'd put Toria on the chair beside me, but the alleged mean-girl tabby jumped up and parked herself on my desk. I gave her a cat toy to play with from the stash I kept in the office, but she was much more interested in sitting on my paperwork and nudging my hand as I tried to work on the computer.

After a bit more work and a lot more cat dodging, I glanced at my watch. I wasn't sure what time it had been when Cash left, but he'd certainly been gone much longer than the twenty to thirty minutes he'd indicated. I would need to get going soon.

I checked my contacts list for a phone number and located Cash's cell.

The call went directly to voice mail.

I'd planned to stop at home to let Dogbert out for a break. Then I had a house call at eleven o'clock with Betty Foxx, who worked for my cousin, Melinda, at her high-end pet shop, the Bow Wow Boutique. I'd been surprised to hear from Betty because my cousin and I were currently on the outs. That's Texan for we aren't speaking to each other.

Like most family disputes it had started over something small—in our case a family brooch. It wasn't that the heirloom piece of jewelry was so valuable, though it was a twenty-two-carat gold basket filled with precious stones. Precious stones shaped like different types of fruit. The brooch was, shall we say, a unique piece of jewelry. The main thing, though, was that our Grandma Tillie had left the brooch to her favorite granddaughter. I knew she meant it to go to me. Mel was just as convinced it was intended for her.

Like I said, you'd think we could work it out, but that ship had long since sailed. Words had been exchanged, not very nice ones, and here we were. The brooch was currently locked up tighter than tight in a safe at my house, but I was sure Mel was trying to figure out how to get it back.

Anyway, needless to say, I had been shocked when Betty phoned and said Melinda had recommended she call me about a problem she was having with her dog. I'd known Betty Foxx from the self-defense class Diana and I had taken, but she'd never mentioned having a dog.

I put the address Betty had given me into my cell phone so I had it for directions and then tried Cash's cell number again. Nothing. Shoot. I needed to get a move on if I was going to make the appointment on time.

I decided I could swing by the house where Cash and Jake lived and drop off Toria. Though brilliant, the two of them were sometimes a little flaky. Just last week the cleaning crew had called because Jake had left his keys in the outer door.

I called Cash's number again and this time left a message letting him know I would drop off Toria at their home. I checked the guys' office for a cat carrier. The computer was still on and I thought about shutting it down, but I hesitated because maybe Cash had intended to leave it on. There was a multi-colored freehand drawing on the back of the screen. It looked like an alien. Sort of a combination of ET's older brother and Munch's eerie painting, "The Scream." Verdi had often complained that she felt creeped out by it when they left their office door open because it was drawn in such a way that it looked like the alien's eyes followed you. The two guys had been amused by her comments.

Now where would they keep a cat carrier?

Found it. The carrier was tucked behind the door. I coaxed Toria into it and then stepped into the reception area, pulled their office door shut, and then closed my own.

Suzanne, the psychic who was one of our officemates, was just arriving. Our Suzanne doesn't look like what you might think of as the stereotypical mind reader. No crystal ball, no long gypsy skirt, no dangly earrings. The lady's look was all business in her tailored dress-for-success black suit, white blouse, and sensible shoes.

She stopped just inside the door and looked at me. Her lips pursed for a moment before she spoke. "What are you doing with the boys' cat?" she asked in her flat, no-nonsense tone.

"Cash left her with me." I held up the carrier. "I'm dropping her off at their house."

"Hmpf. I sense trouble." She turned and walked away.

I didn't know if she meant trouble for me, Jake, Cash, or the cat. Bottom line, I didn't give a lot of credence to the practice of telling the future, but if the woman was going to spout off-the-wall predictions, she ought to be specific.

Seriously, Suzanne? You should have warned me.

Chapter Two

THE HUGE HOUSE where Cash and Jake lived looked more like it belonged on an English estate than on a hill in a California beach town. It certainly was not at all like the many sprawling SoCal-style structures that dominate Laguna's landscape. Their abode was almost castle-like with turrets and towers, and a stone face more reminiscent of moors than beaches. I wasn't sure how they'd gotten the design past the zoning board, but I guess it didn't block any ocean views, which is often the main reason for refusal here in Orange County.

I rang the doorbell and could hear the clanging from inside, but there was no answer. Finally I rapped on the door, though if they hadn't heard the bell, I don't know why I thought they'd hear my knock.

Cash's distinctive red Tesla sports car was parked out front so he had to be inside and must simply be someplace where he couldn't hear the doorbell. I tried the knob and it turned in my hand. Slipping inside, I set the cat carrier on the smooth marble floor and called out.

Unhappy with being home and still caged, Toria meowed in protest.

"Hang on, kitty. Let me check for your people." I walked through the entryway and into the living room.

"Hey, Cash?" I called out again and then walked through toward the kitchen, which I could see was at the back. I looked around, but the place was deserted. Great. Where was he?

The kitchen led to a breakfast area, which in turn opened onto a flagstone patio and a swimming pool that stretched the length of the space. The patio door stood wide open. Ah, this held possibilities.

"Cash? Jake?" I stepped around the massive kitchen table, piled high with electronics, and out into the sunshine. Blinded for a moment by the brightness, I didn't immediately notice the person in the pool.

When I did, I also registered that he was facedown.

Oh, no! Not good.

I kicked my shoes aside and went in. It was a zero-depth pool with a gradual slope leading into the deeper water. But he was clear down in the deep end.

I swam to him, latched onto his shirt. Towed him back to where I could stand. Pulled him to the edge.

His water-logged weight fought me.

Locking my arms under his shoulders, it took several tries, but I finally dragged him up onto the patio. I took in big gulps of air, out of breath from the effort.

Breathe. Get a grip.

I rolled him over and prepared to give CPR. I was rusty, but I'd been trained. I could do this.

As I knelt beside the prone body I realized it wasn't Cash but Jake.

He was fully clothed, jeans, expensive Italian loafers, loud Hawaiian-print shirt.

I also noted drowning was the least of his worries. The blond computer wonder-kid had a power cord wrapped tightly around his neck.

Oh, God. I sent up a swift prayer.

With shaky wet fingers, I loosened the cord, tossed it aside, and checked his neck for a pulse.

Nothing.

I ran back into the house, my wet feet sliding across the wood floor, to where I'd dropped my purse.

I dug out my cell phone and dialed 911.

Chapter Three

"911. WHAT'S YOUR emergency?" a woman answered. I heard her but couldn't form words. I swallowed and tried to speak. My heartbeat pounded in my ears, and I struggled to breathe.

"Three-eight-seven-five de Leon," I finally choked out. "Medical emergency. Drowning. Homicide. I don't know. Just come. Come quick." I knew I wasn't making any sense. "Three-eight-seven-five de Leon." I repeated the address.

"A unit is on its way," replied the crisp voice on the other end.

I ran back to the patio and began chest compressions. Though it seemed like forever before the paramedics came, it probably wasn't. I heard the sirens and then the pounding of feet through the house as they arrived.

I moved out of the way so they could take over, but I could tell from their conversation and lack of action it was no use. They examined Jake, but there was not a life-saving scramble. Not a good sign.

Laguna Beach police officers arrived just behind the medics, and the first responders stepped aside. I'd moved away in order to give them plenty of room.

I know it must seem, at least to those of you who've known me for a while, that I might be a bit desensitized to dead bodies given the fact I've been involved in some previous murder solving. Truth be told, dead bodies are not something you get used to.

Wet and cold, I shivered, even in the heat of the day.

Someone handed me a towel. I looked up.

"Ms. Lamont." Laguna Beach Police Detective Judd Malone and I were on an off-and-on first-name basis. Apparently today was an off day.

"Detective." I took the towel and wrapped it around my shoulders.

"When you called dispatch you mentioned a possible homicide." He was solid and calm in his usual black jeans and black T-shirt.

"Yes. Why?" I tried to keep my voice from shaking.

"Well, this looks like an accidental drowning. Did you think foul play because he was fully clothed?"

I wrapped the towel more tightly around my water-logged self and suddenly thought about Cash. What if he lay dead somewhere else in the house? A home invasion gone wrong perhaps?

"Ms. Lamont?" Malone prompted.

"No, the electrical cord around his neck."

"What cord?" Malone turned his head to look back at Jake's prone body and the paramedics who were packing up their equipment.

I pointed at the cord which lay near a stone flower pot at the fringe of the landscaping. I must have tossed it aside with a little more force than I'd realized.

Malone pivoted. "Hey, hold up." He walked back over to where the medic team surrounded Jake.

I shifted in the deck chair and in doing so knocked a bright-pink energy drink can off the small table. The cold liquid spread across the stone patio under my feet. I mopped at it with my towel.

I have to tell you, I know from previous experience that Detective Judd Malone is very particular about his crime scenes. Not only had I messed with the victim (and the murder weapon), I'd also traipsed through the house itself, dripping water everywhere I went. I had known it was a crime scene, but what was I to do? My phone was in the house, and I'd needed to call in the drowning, er, strangling.

My phone, which I still clutched, suddenly rang.

"Hello?"

"I can't wait here all day, Carol. Your cousin said you were a good pet shrink. She didn't tell me you were a tardy one."

Ah, Betty Foxx. My eleven o'clock appointment.

"It's Caro and I apologize, Betty." I continued to mop at the spilled drink. "I'll call you to reschedule. I've got a bit of an emergency on my hands."

"What kind of emergency?" she snapped. "You—"

"Ms. Lamont, I need to go over some details with you." Malone was back and stood waiting, arms crossed.

"Who's that?" There was nothing wrong with Betty's hearing. "Sounds like that hot homicide detective. Lemme talk to him."

"It's for you." I handed the phone to Malone. Bad, I know, but I figured he'd get her off the phone faster than I could.

"Ms. Lamont can't talk right now." He didn't even wait to see who was on the other end. "She'll call you back when she can." He jabbed the disconnect button and handed me back my cell.

"Thanks." I gave him a weak smile. Where had he been when I'd needed call screening earlier? I'd bet he would've made short work of Geoffrey.

"Now, let's see if you can fill in some blanks for me." Malone planted himself in the chair beside me. "Start at the beginning."

WHEN MALONE WAS done with his questions, I dried my feet, blotting the sticky pink from the spilled drink, and donned my shoes. Then I called and let Betty know I could reschedule our appointment for that afternoon. She was not happy, but there wasn't much I could do about it. Until Malone had said I was free to go, I was pretty much on hold. I think Betty was mostly upset she didn't get the chance to talk directly to Malone.

The place was now crawling with police personnel. They'd gone room to room thoroughly searching the house for Cash, but he was nowhere to be found. I took that as good news. Malone seemed a little more neutral on the subject. He took down Cash's cell-phone number and said they would continue trying to reach him. There was a brief discussion about what should be done with Toria, but really only a cursory one. Detective Malone knew I wasn't going to be okay with sending her to the shelter. Given that Cash was not answering his cell phone, I was drafted as catsitter and was happy to take her with me. It seemed I was free to go.

I stepped outside, cat carrier in hand, and then skidded to a stop.

A crowd had collected in front of the house. In this part of town the houses have some space, but like most of The Hills your neighbors aren't far. I suppose the ambulance and police cars had garnered attention from those who usually either stayed inside or lounged on their own patios.

"What's going on in there, Ms. Lamont?" It was a news reporter with a cameraman in tow. He stuck a microphone in my face.

"Who are you?" I took a step back. I didn't even ask how he knew my name. I have no tolerance for reporters who show up and try to get unsuspecting witnesses to provide a sound bite.

"Callum MacAvoy, Ms. Lamont." His made-for-TV smile came too easy and stayed too long. "May I call you Caro?"

"No, you may not." I glanced around to see how far away my car was and tried to determine if I could get out of the drive without mowing down sightseers.

"Fair enough." He stood down a bit. "So, Ms. Lamont, can you tell us what went on inside this house that brought paramedics, the police, and ultimately the crime-scene van here today."

"No, I can't." I edged away from the camera and his microphone. "You'll have to talk to the police."

"Witnesses say you were the first on the scene."

"What witnesses?" I looked around again. As far as I knew no one had seen me arrive, and I'd called 911 almost immediately. The crowd had continued to grow, maybe thirty to forty people by now. They stood in small groups, talking and staring at the house.

I walked away from the reporter and his microphone. Then I worked my way to my car and excused myself to those who stood behind it, letting them know I would be coming through.

For a moment, I sat there trying to take it in, willing myself to erase Jake's face from my mind's eye. Finally, feeling like I had it together enough to drive, I backed out of the driveway and into the street. Just as I turned the wheel to move forward, Heidi Sussman, Cash's girlfriend, rapped on my window. I pushed the button to roll the window down and talk to her.

"Caro, do you know what's going on?" With her short shorts, spray-on tan, and diamond tennis bracelet, she had sort of a surfer-girl-meets-nouveau-riche look going on. Her unnatural-turquoise eyes blinked furiously. "Is everything okay?"

I paused and sighed. "No, it's not."

"Ohmigod, ohmigod." Heidi's pink, perfectly manicured fingers grabbed her throat. "What's the matter with Ja—? What's going on?"

"Honey, get in the car." I pulled forward a bit and parked at the curb. Heidi came around and slid into the passenger seat.

"I was on my way here when I saw all the people and then I saw the flashing lights and the police." She shook like a nervous Chihuahua.

I placed my hand on her arm. "Listen, hon, something really bad has happened." I swallowed. "Jake has drowned and I don't know where Cash is. I know this is very hard, but you need to talk to the police and let them know anything you can."

"Drowned like he's okay or drowned like he's dead?" She gulped and continued to shake.

"Heidi, hon, Jake is dead." I waited for her to process what I'd just told her. "Had you seen either of them today?"

She twisted the diamond bracelet around and around on her slim wrist and hesitated before answering. "No."

"Did you talk to Cash this morning?" Maybe he'd told her where he was going.

"No, like I said, I was on my way over to swim." At the word "swim" she choked up.

I put my arm around her shoulder as best I could as she took huge gulps of air. After a few minutes, she dabbed at her eyes and pushed her blond hair off of her face.

"Thanks for telling me, Caro. I'm okay."

I dropped her off at her bright-red Escalade Hybrid which was parked a couple of blocks away.

I thought about what she'd said.

Did she truly have no idea where Cash was? And had she been about to ask whether Jake was okay? If so, how had she known it was Jake and not Cash in the house?

I STOPPED BY home to change out of my wet clothes and get Toria settled. My house is pet-friendly so it didn't take a lot to accommodate one more feline. I opened the carrier, and Toria tentatively stepped out. Thelma and Louise didn't exactly roll out the welcome wagon, but there wasn't instant cat smackdown either. That was a good sign.

Clothes changed and animals settled, I packed up and set off for my appointment with Betty Foxx.

The address Betty had given me was inside one of Laguna Beach's gated communities. The entry gate was imposing, the palm trees perfectly spaced, and I knew the real-estate prices had to be as massive as the homes themselves. Once security passed me through, I checked the address and found the house in no time. Or the driveway at least.

I pulled in, followed the long drive, and parked. Betty had apparently been watching for me. She stood out front, attired as usual in pearls and pajamas. Don't ask me. I have no idea why the little lady had decided PJs were daytime attire, but I'd never seen her in anything else. This particular ensemble was vivid green and trimmed in red satin. Perhaps left over from holiday festivities. I parked, got out, and grabbed my bag from the car.

She motioned me toward a smaller stucco guest cottage that was situated behind the larger main house. The big house was grand and imposing, ostentatious and lofty, impressed with itself. The smaller residence was quaint and homey with window boxes overflowing with lush greens and a riot of flowers. Warm, cheerful, cozy. It had all the makings of a traditional grandmother's cottage.

"Is my car okay here?" I turned to ask my not-so-traditional grandmotherly escort. I wasn't sure how long we'd be.

She didn't answer but gave a dismissive Queen Mum wave of her fingers in response.

"Come on." The little elf moved quickly to the steps of the smaller house. She stopped her hand on the doorknob. "We gotta move fast once I open the door. You ready?"

I nodded. The scratching and whining on the other side of the door escalated as she eased it open and popped inside. I followed quickly and then stopped in shock.

The cute cottage looked like it had either hosted rock-and-roll royalty or had been ransacked by a band of robbers. Shoes, clothing, and papers were scattered around the room. A Saint Bernard bounded toward Betty, his excited bark rattling the cups in the nearby antique china hutch.

"Down, Raider," Betty ordered. She reached in her pocket for some treats.

"Down, boy," she tried again. He ignored her and continued barking and jumping on her. I was worried he would knock her down, but her feet were planted firmly apart.

"How long have you had Raider?" I asked.

"Why?" She looked up, raising bright-red eyebrows.

Yes, that's right. Betty's eyebrows were a brilliant shade of red that looked like they'd been drawn on with lipstick. I'd noticed the interesting makeup application when we'd been in self-defense class, but Diana and I had both figured it was best left alone. I mean how do you ask about something like that?

"What does how long I've had the dog have to do with anything?" she demanded.

This was a case that clearly called for directness. "I need to know how long you've been reinforcing bad behavior if I'm going to help you."

"I don't know what you're talking about. He's a good dog." Betty frowned at me.

I crossed my arms and gave her the I-can-wait-you-out look.

She caved. "I've had him for about a month."

"Okay, let's start with when you come home. I'm guessing he's always like this. Right?"

"Yep. He's a high-spirited guy." She smiled and held his big head in her hands.

I thought "high-spirited" was a gross understatement, but I kept my thoughts to myself. Raider was a handsome fellow, and I could see why Betty was enamored with him. Sweet brown eyes looked up at her adoringly, and she seemed completely unbothered by the drool that slipped down his furry chin and onto her thumbs.

"The first thing we'll need to work on is absolutely no treats for him when he's in a hyper-excited state." I held out my hand for the treats, and she reluctantly handed them over. "He only gets these as a reward for when he's calm." I walked across the room and picked up things from the floor as I went. "Okay?"

"Okay, fine."

"And Betty?" I turned and leaned down to look her in the eye. "Raider has to get some exercise. A big part of his problem is that he's still a pup and he's got to have some way to expend all this energy."

"Hmmm . . ." Her eyes dropped.

"If you don't feel you're up to walking him, I could suggest a couple of very dependable dog-walkers. Shall we take him outside for a little walk right now?"

"No." Her answer came back too quickly. "He's been out. I took him when I was waiting for you. Just tell me what I need to do. I'll take care of it."

"First, you'll need to make sure that he gets exercised every single day. Second, no dog treats when he's in an excited state. Raider is going to eventually be even bigger than he is, and if you're going to manage this dog you've got to get control now. What is he, a little over a year old?"

"Eighteen months." She patted Raider's head and then leaned down to place a kiss on top of his massive crown. "And I am keeping him. No one is taking him away."

I felt my heart tighten. I had to find a way to help the little stubborn lady. I understood the attachment, but I was seriously convinced there was a good chance the dog would eventually injure her if she didn't get the situation under control.

"What were you doing with Detective Hot Stuff?" She wiggled crimson brows. "I thought Cookie said you were engaged to the Greek. You two-timing him?"

By "Cookie" I knew she meant my cousin, Melinda. When we were in the self-defense class, Betty had always referred to Mel as "Cookie."

And the "Greek" she referred to was Sam Gallanos, who I was not engaged to, much to my mother's disappointment.

"Sam?" I sighed. "We're not engaged. We're just . . ." I hesitated. Why was I explaining to Betty my relationship with Sam? "Anyway, my interaction with Detective Malone wasn't social. It was business."

"A murder then?" She continued to pat Raider's head, and he settled against her legs. "Who died? Why were you there?"

The bright-green pixie was full of questions.

"I discovered the body." I stopped. Surely the story would be on the news, and I hadn't been asked to keep anything confidential. But it seemed wrong to share too much info. "It was someone I knew."

I continued to pick up items from the floor as we talked. I absent-mindedly sorted them into recognizable and no-longer-recognizable categories.

"Where did you get that red hair? I thought you and Cookie were related." Betty looked up from where she now sat on the floor. Raider licked her face, leaving a trail of slobber, but she didn't seem to mind.

"We are. Our mothers are sisters." Melinda was a gorgeous brunette with smooth dark hair I'd always envied. "I think one of my great-aunts was a redhead."

"How come you two don't just call a truce? You've got your granny's pin, right?"

"I do." She referred, of course, to the family brooch I'd mentioned earlier. "Well . . ." I hesitated and bent to pick up a colorful rag that looked like it might have once been a piece of clothing.

How could I explain two grown women in a battle over an ugly piece of jewelry? Better people (or at least people with more clout) than Betty had attempted to convince us to stand down on the Brooch Wars, but neither of us could see a way for a win-win. Someone would have to be the loser. Not happening.

As I straightened, I noticed Betty slip Raider a treat. It was clear she'd only turned over part of her doggie-treat stash.

Seriously? How could I help her and Raider if she refused to be honest?

"Betty?" I waited until she made eye contact. "I'm not the treat police, but if you continue to give your dog treats at inappropriate times, you aren't going to be able to control him, and you'll end up losing him. I don't think that's what you want. Is it?" I held her gaze, and suddenly her snappy blue eyes misted over.

"No, it isn't." Her voice quavered, and that was almost my undoing.

I sat down beside her on the floor and patted Raider's big head.

"Hon, it's just like raising a child. You can love them with all your heart, but you have to set boundaries and not over-indulge them or you'll end up with a spoiled brat."

Betty muttered a comment. It sounded like she said, "Amen to that." But I couldn't quite hear as she was struggling to stand.

"Okay, Caramel." She popped up in front of me. "I'll hold back on the spoiling."

"It's Caro," I automatically corrected. "All right then, let's make a deal.

You start with the exercise and no treats when Raider is excited." I handed her my card. "Call me if you need anything."

"Okey dokey, Carol." She tucked the card in her pocket.

I sighed. It didn't really matter what she called me as long as she did as I asked. "I'll check back later in the week to see how you're doing."

I sincerely hoped Betty would make the effort. Raider was a sweet dog, but it was going to take a lot of time to work with him and get his behavior under control. And the rambunctious pup would easily end up at one-hundred-and-fifty pounds, perhaps more, when he was full grown.

I'd seen it before. These types of situations could go both ways. It was all about commitment.

I had dinner plans with "The Greek" as Betty had called him, but I had one stop I needed to make before heading home to get ready for the evening.

I parked in the adjoining lot and ducked into Coast Hardware. There might be fancier coffeemakers available elsewhere, but I wasn't picky. A basic coffeepot would do the trick.

One thing I knew for sure, I abso-dang-lutely was *not* going to face another day without my morning coffee.

Chapter Four

AFTER A REALLY bad day, a quiet dinner with Sam Gallanos was just what the doctor ordered.

The restaurant was top drawer and the company even better. Bistro A was a new Orange-County hot spot with locally grown veggies and fresh California seafood. And Sam Gallanos was the perfect company, the perfect date, and the perfect friend. It was what went beyond friendship that I just couldn't seem to commit to. Sam had made it clear he wanted to be more. He'd even taken me to meet his grandmother. A big step in his world.

Sam's grandparents had raised him after his mother and stepfather were killed in a car accident. The grands dealt in olives, his stepfather had dealt in movies, and his birth father was never talked about. Though his grandfather had been gone for years, from Sam's accounts Dorothea, his grandmother, had always run the olive import/export business. She was still very involved but was transitioning much of the day-to-day affairs to Sam. Dark eyes and hair, like Sam, she was ageless and sharp; he called her *Yia-Yia* which he pronounced *Ya-Ya*. I had loved her at first sight.

The bistro's décor was trendy but crisp and clean. Pacific blues and greens blended with cloth-covered tables arranged around a trickling fountain and a large, vivid cobalt-colored burst of glass reminiscent of Dale Chihuly's blown-glass sculptures. With the natural light and subtle focus lighting, it was somehow both striking and soothing.

We were seated almost immediately, but I still could sense heads turn as the maître d' led us to our table. Sam had that effect on a room.

Don't get me wrong; I know I don't exactly blend into the background. I'm a tall redhead, and my days on the beauty pageant-circuit had left me with great runway posture. And my new deep-navy Jenny Packham dress was nice. Sleek, sleeveless, slimming. But, make no mistake, it was my date who created the stir. Sam was drop-dead (if you'll pardon the term) handsome and always put together like he'd just walked off the pages of a magazine.

Tall and athletic with dark-brown hair and even darker eyes, Sam Gallanos never failed to draw the gaze of every female, from eighteen to eighty. It would be as irritating as a heat rash if it weren't for the fact that he was totally oblivious to it.

Sam selected wine, and we took recommendations for our entrees from the waiter who struck the perfect balance between attentive but unobtrusive. Once we'd ordered, Sam asked about Jake, and I described the scene I'd found when I'd arrived.

When I'd finished he reached over and covered my hand with his. "Caro, *hrisu mou*, that must have been awful." Sam occasionally lapsed into his native Greek. Sometimes I asked for translation, other times not. You know, it had been truly awful, and I was glad to finally share with someone else how horrible it had been.

As we turned our conversation to other things I felt myself relax. I asked Sam about his grandmother and how his new role in the company was working out. We discussed his upcoming business trip to the Bay Area.

I explained about my failed coffeepot and the new one I'd purchased this afternoon. Sam laughed out loud when I described my visit to Betty's cottage and the challenge the combination of one senior and one soon-to-be huge dog presented. I asked about Sam's dog Mac. Border Collies are one of my favorite breeds, and Mac is one of my favorite Border Collies. We made plans to get Mac and Dogbert together for a beach playdate in a couple of days.

When my phone rang, I picked it up to turn the sound off. If it was a client, it could wait. If it was my mama with more family reunion plans, she could wait.

I glanced at the number.

Okay, this was the one call that couldn't wait. A sense of relief washed over me. It was Graham Cash.

"Excuse me," I said to Sam, and quickly pushed the button.

"Boy, am I glad to hear from you." I wasn't going to waste time with hello.

"I'm not supposed to be making phone calls." His voice was barely above a whisper. "If they find out, I'm dead meat."

What? Had Cash been kidnapped?

"Wait a minute." I pressed the phone to my ear. "Where are you?"

"I can't say," he spoke quickly. "I got your message about Jake not picking up Toria, and I just wanted to make sure kitty's okay."

"No problem there. She's fine, but—"

Cash cut me off. "Oh, good. Gotta go."

"But—" The phone was dead. I looked at it. Looked at Sam. Looked back at the phone. I felt panic rise in my throat at the implications of Cash's call.

"Caro, what is it? Is something wrong?" Sam's deep-brown eyes searched my face. "Your family?"

"No, nothing like that." I shook my head. "That was Graham Cash and he couldn't talk. He wanted to check on his cat."

"It's good that you heard from him, right?" The furrow in his forehead deepened with concern.

"Yes and no. We now know he's not dead but he sounded like he might be being held against his will." I didn't even question the fact that I used "we" as if it were partly my investigation. "Sam, excuse me for a second, I've got to let Detective Malone know about the call."

I stepped outside to call Malone, but my call, of course, went to voice mail. It wasn't that I expected the homicide detective to work 24/7, but it seemed I always got his voice mail. I left a message to let him know I'd heard from Cash and repeated the call as I remembered it, then returned to the table.

Our dinner had arrived, but the luscious food, the quietly chic ambiance, the carefully selected wine, were wasted on me. All I could think about was the phone call from Cash.

I picked at my food, the tension back, my appetite gone.

"Ready to go?" Sam clearly sensed my distraction and to his considerable credit understood.

I nodded, and he signaled for the check.

The drive back to my place was quiet. Sam's light-blue Ferrari hummed down Coast Highway hugging the roadway gently on the turns, and we let the quiet settle between us. I appreciated time to simply enjoy the view (both of the Pacific and of Sam) and tried to push aside the picture of Jake Wylie I couldn't seem to get out of my head.

SAM PULLED INTO my driveway, turned off the engine, and came around the car to open my door. The sky was a beautiful shade of deep peach and cranberry, and the waning sunset cast shadows on the facade of my house. Maybe that's why I didn't immediately see the guy sitting on my front step.

As we walked to the door, a figure stood, and I felt Sam's arm around my waist tense.

The man stepped forward.

"Hello, Carolina." Geoffrey was still tall, dark, and handsome, if you'll pardon the cliché. The suave masculinity remained, but the polished good looks that used to make me weak-kneed now did nothing for me at all.

Sam stepped forward, essentially cutting between us. "You are?"

"Geoffrey Carlisle." He extended his hand. "I'm Carolina's husband."

As he said my name his familiarity washed over me like an unwelcome caress. "Ex-husband," I corrected.

"Of course," he said smoothly. "And you are?"

"Sam Gallanos." Sam shook Geoff's hand.

I liked that Sam didn't have to add a tagline that claimed me like property. Still his posture said he'd step in if needed.

"What are you doing here, Geoff?"

"As I said when we talked, I was in the area."

Oh yeah, when we talked. That would be when he called and wanted to get together and I said no and hung up on him. The man lived in an alternate universe where everything revolved around him.

I was working on forming all of that into a sentence that left no doubt he needed to be on his way, but didn't make me sound like a complete crazy shrew, when another car pulled up. It was Detective Malone.

He joined the group, his eyes sliding from Sam to Geoff to me.

"Everything okay, Ms. Lamont?"

There was nothing I'd learned in all those etiquette classes I'd had to attend in my pageant days that covered the rules on properly introducing your ex-husband to your current beau, and then to the local homicide detective. Nothing at all that covered proper form for that type of introduction.

I opted for names only.

"Detective Malone, Geoffrey Carlisle. Geoff, Judd Malone. And you already know Sam."

Geoff stared a hole right through me, his eyes accusing. I felt anxiousness rise up in me, though I knew he no longer had anything at all to do with me or my life.

Suddenly it hit me. He thought I'd somehow called the police. Of course he did, because it's always all about him.

I looked away from Geoff, and my eyes landed on Sam. His expression said it all, and in that moment I think I fell in love with Sam just a little more. He didn't have to say a word. Sam trusted me to handle the situation, and he had my back. If I needed him he was there. Solid and strong, but he believed in me enough to let me be strong on my own.

I turned to Malone. "Do you have my house under surveillance?"

He had the grace to look a little guilty but just barely. "We're keeping an eye on things, in case Graham Cash decides to come for his cat."

"So that's a yes."

He didn't respond.

"All I can tell you about his call is exactly what I told you in the message I left for you." I pulled my cell from my evening bag. "The call was from his usual number, he said he couldn't talk, 'they' would kill him, and he didn't give me time to ask if he knew about Jake."

"You're welcome to check my phone if you like." I handed it to Malone.

He looked at the call record and handed it back.

"If that's all?"

"It is." He nodded.

"Then, gentlemen, I'm done. I've had a stressful day and I'm going in."

Malone stood arms crossed and stared at Geoffrey. Geoff finally caved and moved to leave, but as he passed by, he angled his body in front of me and paused.

"I'll phone you tomorrow," he said quietly.

I wasn't going to dignify that volley with a response. I hoped my in-your-dreams glare left no doubts.

Detective Malone still hadn't moved.

"If you hear from Graham Cash . . ."

"I know, call you."

Malone headed back to his car.

Sam walked me to the door and waited for me to use my key.

"Call me if you need anything." He kissed me and then tipped my head back to look into my eyes. "I have to say, Caro Lamont, you lead one helluva complicated life."

I slipped inside, locked the door, and leaned my forehead against it. *Whoo boy. You ain't just whistling Dixie.*

After all the testosterone had left the building, or in this case my front step, I greeted my menagerie and flipped on some lights. I changed into comfy yoga pants and made myself a cup of tea. I'd just parked myself in my favorite chair with a book when my phone trilled "Deep in the Heart of Texas."

Yeah, as if the day hadn't already been stressful enough. The unique ring told me the caller was the one person in the world who knew how to push all my buttons.

"Hello, Mama."

Now with some mothers it might be possible to delay a lengthy discussion by simply saying, "Mama, I've had a tough day. Can we talk later?"

But not my mama. Katherine Lamont neé Montgomery was like a dog with a bone when an idea took hold of her. In the passionate throes of planning an event, nothing dissuaded her from talking to you when *she* wanted to talk to you.

Her idea du jour was a big ole Texas barbecue combined with a Montgomery family reunion. I was very much afraid she and Barbara, Melinda's mother, had cooked up the idea with the goal of patching up things between Mel and me. It was to be at the family homestead, the Montgomery Ranch, this summer. She tossed out some potential dates, and I told her I'd have to get back to her.

I did mention the fact I'd found a dead body in the course of my day, but avoided most of the details. Especially details that might have her getting on a plane to make sure I was okay.

She acknowledged that was an upsetting state of affairs. But once she'd confirmed I was okay and it didn't involve anyone she knew, she was back to planning activities and menus. It's not so much that Mama Kat is heartless or shallow, it's just that she's focused. At least that's what I assured myself as she went on about brisket and potato salad.

Finally, she wound down and I promised I would check the dates she'd given me and get back to her within a few days.

With Mama off the phone, I wandered through my house picking up the remnants of the day. I picked up pillows my pet roommates had knocked off the couch, gathered papers to go into the recycling, set my useless coffeepot in the garage, and set the new one on the kitchen counter, too tired to deal with it right then.

I washed my face, brushed my teeth, crawled into bed, and said a short prayer for Graham Cash, wherever he was. I hoped the young Brit was safe. In short order I was joined by both Dogbert and Toria. Dogbert settled in his usual spot against the back of my knees, and I cuddled the soft tabby against me.

"We'll sort this out tomorrow." I patted her head. "I'm sure he hasn't deserted you."

She purred, and Dogbert snuggled in agreement.

Chapter Five

THE NEXT MORNING I plugged in my brand new coffeemaker with high hopes. I'd intended to unpack it and give it a trial run last night, but after all the excitement on my front doorstep I just plain hadn't had it in me. Once I'd gotten Mama off the phone, I'd been too darn tired to do much of anything.

As I let the coffee brew, I flipped on the television and tuned it to the local news. There was an overnight house fire in Newport, a high-surf warning, something about a protest at Main Beach involving some housing project, and then the picture switched to the scene at Jake and Cash's house yesterday.

There was a clear shot of water-logged me as I tried to get to my car holding Toria's cat carrier. I looked both ways as if looking for an escape route, and I guess I had been. Then the reporter (I couldn't remember his name) asked, "So, Ms. Lamont, can you tell us what went on inside this house that brought paramedics, the police, and ultimately the crime-scene van here today."

"No, I can't," TV me replied.

It seemed beyond callous to worry about your appearance at the scene of a murder, but I have to tell you I looked like I'd been chewed up, spit out, and stepped on. My lovely Akris crepe tunic was a dried mess of wrinkled white cotton, my hair was a tangled mess of red frizz that looked like something out of the *Bride of Frankenstein*, and I had more mascara on my cheeks than on my eyelashes. Thank God, my mama hadn't seen the news clip or I'd never hear the end of it.

I poured a cup of coffee, inhaling the soothing aroma, and mulled the crazy events of yesterday. It seemed like several days ago rather than just one. Who had killed Jake and why? And where was Cash?

On auto-pilot I filled dog and cat dishes with food and water. Thelma and Louise came immediately to check their provisions for the day. Toria followed behind.

My cell phone rang, and the distinctive ring gave away the caller's identity. I sighed.

"Hello again, Mama."

"Carolina, have you seen the news?" She was out of breath as if she'd been on a mile run and was about to faint.

I assumed that meant the news clip had been picked up by at least one of the national networks. I imagined that would make Mr. TV Reporter happy. He'd seemed like someone that would matter to.

Mama Kat didn't wait for my answer. "My word, Caro, what happened to you? You look like something the cat dragged in."

"Mama, a man was dead. I didn't have time to worry about how I looked."

"I understand a man was dead, but my goodness, child, you have to think about how you present yourself. It appears there were a lot of people there and now it's on the TV news everywhere."

I thought "everywhere" might be a gross exaggeration.

"I was just trying to get to my car, Mama. I had no idea there would be this big crowd or a reporter with a camera. My concern was a man was dead."

"No matter what, you've always got to be aware and be prepared," she intoned in a low serious voice, like it was the Southern Girl's Code of Honor or something. And maybe it was. I have to tell you, Mama Kat never went anywhere without a can of hairspray and a tube of lipstick.

"Got it." There was no point in arguing. I'd already mentioned a couple of times the fact there was a dead guy.

"Okay, honey-bun, you take care and don't be talking on camera without freshening up a bit. Love you. Bye."

And she was gone.

I poured another cup of coffee and went to get ready for the day. I heard my mama's voice in my head as I dressed, but I still chose jeans and a casual top. My profession often requires me to chase an uncooperative canine, or crouch down and get eye to eye with a determined doggie. It wasn't that I'd lost all my fashion sense, I still enjoyed getting duded up for a night out, and surely I should get major points for the stylish Jenny Packham I'd worn last night. But during the day my selections were based on practicality and comfort. I pulled on my favorite True Religion jeans and a navy Donna Karan asymmetrical top. Fun, fashionable, but still functional.

Okay, I confess I did a quick check of my makeup before I left. And all right, full confession, I threw an extra lipstick in my bag.

MY FIRST STOP of the day was a couple who'd adopted a young beagle after the loss of their longtime family dog who had also been a beagle. So Nick and Bonnie Humphries were familiar with the breed. Beagles are fun and loving companions but can also be stubborn and difficult to train. Although it had been a while since they'd had a young dog, I didn't get the impression that they were unrealistic in what was required to train a beagle.

I was pretty darn sure a dark-colored SUV had been on my tail all the way to the Humphries home. Malone had said the police were watching my house, but he hadn't mentioned anything about them following me. With a sense of unease, I stopped before turning in and waited. But the SUV didn't hesitate; it drove right on by.

I parked in the driveway and reviewed my notes. The issue was that Rosie was howling. Now, howling is not unusual for a beagle, but Rosie was howling so loudly when they took her for walks sometimes people would come out of their houses to see what was going on. Bonnie said she thought some concerned citizens actually thought they might be abusing the dog. Nothing could be further from the truth; the two always took great care of Rosie.

I grabbed my bag and climbed the steps to the wraparound porch. The house was a well-kept California cottage-style home. I admired the big Lilac Godetia plant that spilled over onto the decking. My friend Diana had introduced me to the lavender-shaded blooms, though she called the plant Farewell-to-Spring. Seeing the flowers reminded me: she and I were due for a lunch. She'd undoubtedly also seen the morning news, but unlike Mama Kat would be less worried about my fashion sense and more concerned about my mental state. I should call her and let her know I was okay.

"Good morning." Bonnie answered the door immediately. Nick stood just inside, Rosie at his side.

"How are you and how is Rosie?" I asked the two.

"We're doing well and Rosie is improving," Bonnie answered.

"That's great." I smiled and waited for Bonnie to go on. Rosie patiently sat beside Nick, her eyes watching me intently. I'd be willing to bet she remembered I was the lady with the homemade dog treats.

"We saw you on the news this morning." Nick stepped forward.

Why had it not occurred to me that if my mother in Texas had seen the television spot, all of my clients would have seen it as well? I could understand they'd be curious, but still I hated the idea of talking about it.

"A sad situation," I said. "I hope the police find out what happened."

I asked if we could get Rosie's leash and take a walk around the neighborhood while we discussed what they'd been working on. I kept the conversation directed to Rosie's behavior. I also kept an eye out for the dark-colored vehicle, and thought I spotted the back of it once turning the corner. But when we reached the cross-street there was no dark SUV in sight.

After the walk and talking a little bit more with Bonnie and Nick, it seemed to me Rosie was simply doing what beagles do. They're bred to use their noses to track. Rosie was a good detective. She was tracking and finding and letting them know. I suggested some in-the-yard games where Rosie could use her extra-sensitive nose to find things. Also, I suggested a few things to keep her on track during walks.

Promising to check in with the couple in a week to follow up on Rosie's progress, I packed up. Back at my car, I glanced around again before getting in, but the dark SUV I thought had been following me when I'd arrived was nowhere in sight. It had probably been a product of my over-active imagination.

I didn't have another client until afternoon so I took the opportunity to call the police and ask if it would be possible for me to collect some of Toria's things from Cash and Jake's house. I had cat food and feline treats, but I thought it might make things easier for her if she had some of her own things.

I was put through to Detective Malone who thankfully didn't give me any grief. He said he would have an officer meet me there. I didn't know how long I would have Toria, but I wasn't handing her over to animal control. I truly believed Cash would be back for his cat. After all he'd cared enough to call and make sure she was alright.

The beautiful tabby seemed to be okay at my house. She and Dogbert had come to an understanding yesterday, and Thelma and Louise had decided they would tolerate her. In fact, my new furry resident seemed to be much more of a cuddler than my two felines. Last night she and Dogbert had competed for lap time.

I swung by my house to pick up Toria. I thought taking her with me might be a good idea. That way if I had trouble picking favorite toys or treats, she could weigh in with her opinion.

As I made my way to Cash and Jake's house, I was sure I spotted the dark-colored SUV again in my rearview mirror. I couldn't tell if the color was dark blue or black, and, in truth, I couldn't be sure it was the same vehicle I'd seen earlier. I slowed down and reached for my cell phone, but when I looked again it was gone.

I pulled up in front of the house and parked. I felt my stomach muscles clench. The storybook exterior belied the tragedy that had happened within its walls.

Cash's red Tesla still sat out front, the sleek car gleaming in the sunlight. A Laguna Beach blue and white was parked beside it, and a uniformed officer got out as soon as I parked. As promised, Malone had sent an officer to meet me and let me into the house. It was just my luck it was young and earnest Officer Hostas. We'd met before under some interesting circumstances in the course a previous investigation. His set jaw told me he remembered me.

Officer Serious unlocked the door and held it so I could step inside. I set Toria's carrier on the floor in the entryway, and Officer Hostas chatted with her while I walked through. He seemed to like the cat better than he liked me.

I looked around. Needless to say, the day of the murder I hadn't really stopped to admire the opulent interior. The first room I walked into was a wonderful airy room with large, solid pieces of furniture that seemed at once both expensive and comfortable. It reminded me of a Victorian drawing room but for the lived-in look of computers, magazines, and empty snack-food bags scattered about. Thinking a cupboard where the full bags of snacks were kept might also be a promising place for cat food, I moved on to the kitchen.

The table was still stacked with electronics. I wondered what on earth the two techies had been working on that required what looked, to me at least, to be enough computer gear to power a town.

A pantry off the kitchen area held bachelor staples: jars of salsa, bags of chips, and meals-in-a-box. However, the bottom shelf was dedicated to special cat food, deluxe cat treats, and feline vitamin supplements. I picked them up and carried them back the living room placing them by my bag. I was sure there were kitty toys somewhere else in the house.

Officer Hostas had taken Toria from the carrier and was holding her. I didn't blame him; the friendly feline was hard to resist. He petted her head, and she leaned against his chest, sending him adoring looks. I could hear her purring from across the room.

"I'm going to go through here and see if I can find her toys." I indicated a wide opening that looked like it led to a combination family/theater room which was a couple of steps down.

"That's fine," he responded. "The house has been cleared. Crime-scene team is completely done."

As I stepped down into the family room, I caught my foot on a cord. Bang! A stack of equipment fell, and the loud noise echoed through the house. I dashed back to the living room.

Startled, Toria leapt from Officer Hostas's arms leaving a stripe of red angry scratches.

He let go of her, and the cat pushed off his midsection and shot across the room, a grey streak of fur. Up the stairs she went in a matter of seconds. We followed on her heels, er, paws, but she was too fast.

At the landing she hesitated and turned to look at us, her worried green eyes round with fear. Then she scampered up the rest of the stairs, her short legs and wide low-to-the-ground body gone in a flash.

Once at the top, I looked both ways but didn't spot her. Super. Most of the rooms' doors were open, so who knew where the little minx had gone?

Hostas was right behind me. I noticed the blood on his arm. "Are you okay?"

"I'm fine." He dabbed at it, but the skin around the line of scratches was beginning to swell.

"Are you allergic?"

"No, not that I know of." His tone was abrupt.

"Well, in any case, let's get this washed off and then we'll find the runaway kitty." I stepped to the next doorway. "Surely one of these leads to a bathroom."

"I'm fine. There's soap in the kitchen. I'll rinse it off." He glared at me as if I were to blame, and I guess indirectly I was. "Let me know when you've found the cat."

"Will do." I smiled weakly and turned back to the hallway.

I began a systematic search of the second floor. In each room, I looked under the beds and behind the curtains, calling Toria the whole time. The rooms, like the downstairs, were furnished with large, dark-wood furniture. Bedspreads were brocade but in deep, solid, masculine colors.

I finished one side of the hall and started down the other.

"Have you found the cat?" Hostas called from downstairs.

"No," I yelled back.

I could hear Officer Hostas's cell phone ring, and he answered. "No, we're not quite done. The cat escaped and the pet shrink is looking for it. I'll be there as soon as I can." His irritated voice got closer as he climbed the stairs.

"You can go if you need to." I poked my head out from the bedroom I was searching. "I'll keep looking until I find her."

I could tell he was torn. "There's a protest at Main Beach that's maxed our uniformed resources."

"Go." I tried hard to look responsible. "I'll find the cat and lock up."

"All right." He'd wrapped a dish towel around his shredded arm. "Make sure the front door is locked. I'll take the keys with me."

Once he was gone I continued combing through the remaining rooms, still checking under beds and still calling Toria.

"Here, Toria. Here, kitty, kitty." There was no sign of her at all. Maybe she'd somehow gone back downstairs. I stood in the hallway and listened.

Wait a minute. I could hear a faint meow. I moved quietly up and down the hallway attempting to figure out where the sound was coming from. It was slightly louder toward the far end of the hallway where there was another set of stairs. I slowly climbed the short flight, but once at the top could no longer hear the soft mewling.

At the top of the stairs was the turret room. I peered in, fascinated with the round tower-like room. Then I came back down, one step at a time. I stopped and listened on each step. And then back up, continuing to listen. I stepped inside the room. It was filled with all sorts of interesting gadgets, as well as a shiny telescope and shelves that should have held books but instead held more gadgets. There was a massive round computer desk in the center of the room.

"Toria? Here, kitty," I called.

Finally in frustration I sat down at the desk and listened.

"Meow." There. I could hear her.

I stood, and as I did the wall beside me soundlessly slid open.

Toria shot out of the open wall and leapt into the middle of the desk, sliding across the papers and scattering them on the floor. I opened my mouth to scream, but nothing came out.

Then a man stepped out of the open wall.

This time I did scream, the sound echoing in the high-ceilinged room.

"Who are you?" he demanded.

I could barely hear him over the sound of my heart pounding in my ears. He was skinny and not very tall, but his blond hair was wild and his face bright red which somehow made him seem more menacing. He held a small, black metal box.

"The question is who are you?" I shot back. Was I face to face with Jake's murderer? I automatically felt my jeans pocket for my cell phone, but then, with a sinking feeling, remembered it was downstairs with my bag. I was really sorry I'd sent Officer Hostas on his way.

"I'm no one you need to concern yourself with."

"This is a crime scene and there's an officer downstairs," I bluffed.

"No, there's not." He shook his shaggy head. "I saw him drive away."

Toria walked back and forth on top of the desk and meowed at us as if mediating.

Well, good news, I guess. The cat was found.

"How did you get in that room?" I pointed at the wall that gaped open and the space I could see beyond. I also eased myself from behind the desk and closer to the door, hoping he didn't notice my movement. I had no cell phone and no weapon. I would have to make a run for it.

"Stop," he ordered, and I flinched. The guy didn't seem to have a weapon, just that small box, but the image of Jake with the computer cord around his neck was burned into my memory.

"What were you doing in there?" I squared my shoulders and asked. Meanwhile, my eyes searched the room for any sort of object I could use to slow him down. There was the telescope which I was sure would be pretty heavy. And all those gadgets on the shelves might work if I could hurl one of them just right.

"Listen, lady. I don't know what you're doing here, but you need to mind your own business."

"I'm just the catsitter." Maybe if he thought I was no threat he wouldn't kill me.

He nodded as if somehow that fact really did let me off the hook, then suddenly he turned, tucked whatever it was he'd taken under his arm, and brushing past me, ran from the room.

I heard his feet pound on the stairs as he went down and then heard the front door slam. I know I should have followed him, but my whole body was frozen in place by my narrow escape. I hurried to the window. He ran to a small, white sports car parked in front of the house next door and sped away. I was too far away to see the make and model. The car had California plates, but I couldn't see the license number.

I stumbled to the desk and collapsed into the chair. My gaze was drawn to the small secret room beyond the open wall. There were shelves of what looked to be additional electronics. It looked to me like stereo receivers, but I'm betting that wasn't what they were.

I hurried downstairs, glanced out the front door, and then locked it. I know it sounds silly with people popping out of walls, but it made me feel safer. I picked up my tote which was by the door where I'd left it. Then fishing my cell phone from my bag, I dialed Detective Malone.

"Hello?" Malone answered immediately.

I found my lips quivering, but I gripped the phone tighter and made myself explain what had just transpired. I could tell Malone was a bit irritated that Officer Hostas had not stayed with me.

"I'll send an officer over," he said.

"Do I need to stay?" I was already late for an appointment with a new client. I hadn't planned on my stop for Toria's things to take so long, and I needed to take her back to my house before I met with the client. And, to tell you the truth, I wasn't wild about sticking around alone in the empty house.

"Go ahead and leave, but lock up. We've got all personnel on duty tied up right now but we'll check it out. I'll get your statement later."

"Okay, thanks." I noted Toria on the stairs watching me. I grabbed the bag of treats and shook a few in my hand. She trotted right over.

Brilliant. Why hadn't I thought of the treats earlier?

I put Toria into her carrier so she didn't take off again. Then I went to re-stack the equipment I'd knocked over. I don't think I'd ever seen so many computers in one place, short of a big-box store. Once I'd cleaned up my mess, gathered my things to leave, I locked the door and pulled it shut, and then transferred the carrier and Toria's things to my vehicle.

As I walked around to get in my car, I noticed the next-door neighbor, a tall thin man, standing in his front yard. It was a big house also, though less imposing than Jake and Cash's. Still, any property in this part of town, you were talking millions. Seeing me, he bent to pull some weeds from the large planter near the stone walkway.

I walked over to the sturdy stone and wrought-iron fence that surrounded the property, but he turned to leave as I got close.

"Hey," I called. "Did you see the guy that was just here?"

The man didn't look up. "No, I was busy." His dark dress pants and blue-striped Brooks Brothers' shirt seemed like odd attire for yard work.

"He was in that white sports car that just drove away."

He raised his gaze from the flowers, his thin face expressionless. "Didn't see it."

"Fine." There was no way he could have missed it if he'd been outside.

"What are you doing in there?" He pointed at the house.

"Just picking up some things for Toria, Graham Cash's cat."

"She's vicious." His hard tone matched his expression.

"What?" I was taken aback by his vehemence. "No, she's not." Though I thought maybe Officer Hostas might disagree. Still she'd only scratched him because she'd been startled by the noise I caused when I'd knocked over the computer equipment.

"I hope you take that nasty creature away from here and never bring it back." He stomped to his front door, went inside, and closed the door with a heavy clank.

Well, heck, not everyone is a cat fan.

I shook my head. What had started out as a mission to pick up some cat food and a few kitty toys had turned into quite an adventure with an injured officer, a secret room, a strange intruder, and an even stranger neighbor. I wondered what the man did for a living. Jake and Cash's neighborhood wasn't exactly working class.

I got in my car and put it in gear to back out.

Toria stuck a paw through the carrier door, and said, "Meow!" with a decidedly irritated tone.

"I know, girlfriend." I patted her paw. "I'm with you. Something is not right."

Chapter Six

I CALLED OLIVIA, the client I'd been supposed to meet, and apologized. She was very understanding and more than willing to reschedule. I was relieved because having a guy walk out of a wall unexpectedly had thrown me for a loop, and then my interaction with Jake and Cash's neighbor had heaped on more unease. At the moment I was having trouble keeping my mind in the game.

After dropping Toria off at my house and taking Dogbert for a short walk, I felt a little more composed. I picked up my to-do list and my bag. I hoped I'd be able to concentrate once I got to the office.

My stomach growled as I drove past Green's Deli, and I took that as a signal I should turn in. You'd think all the stress of the past two days would have caused me to lose my appetite, but it doesn't work that way with me.

A parking spot opened up in front of the deli, and I parked and grabbed my handbag. They had the best pastrami sandwiches in miles, and while I'm partial to a chocolate éclair from C'est la Vie when I'm stressed, Green's pastrami was a close second.

As I reached the deli's entrance, I could almost taste the Swiss cheese and peppery-rub combination that made the sandwich special. Suddenly the glass-plated door opened and Heidi Sussman stepped out. Dressed in her usual pseudo-surfer-girl couture, she held a deli sack and a drink.

"Hello, Heidi." I couldn't imagine. In the space of one day, to have someone you were close to die and, on top of it, someone you cared about missing and under suspicion for the friend's death. "How are you holding up?"

"I'm okay." Her brightly colored tropical sundress set off her petite stature, her blond hair, and her trim figure. "How about you?"

"Well, since you ask." I blew out a breath. "I have to tell you I've just had quite a scare."

"What do you mean?" She took a big gulp from the open energy drink can she held.

"I'm really glad I ran into you." We stepped to the side so others could enter the deli. "I'd like to ask you about a couple of things."

"Me, really? What about?"

"I was at Cash and Jake's house today to get some of Toria's things."

"I thought no one was allowed in there," she interrupted.

"I had permission from the police, and an officer went with me," I explained. "While I was there, this guy appeared from a hidden space in the turret room."

"I thought you were just there to get stuff for the cat?"

"I was, but I had Toria with me and she got loose and I had to find her." It seemed to me Heidi was distracted. "Do you know anything about this hidden room?"

"No, they were both pretty secretive about their work though."

I hadn't said it had anything to do with their work, but okay.

"So you didn't know about it?"

"No." She moved to leave. "I have to get back to work."

"One more thing. When I left, the next-door neighbor was outside. Tall and thin, I didn't catch his name, but he sure wasn't very friendly."

"No, he's a kook. He claimed Cash's cat was vicious and got into his yard and bit him."

"I can't imagine Toria doing that."

So the unfriendly neighbor I'd talked to was also the person who had accused Toria of bad behavior.

"No, neither could Cash. He hardly ever lets the cat out of the house. Maybe out on the patio but that's all. The weirdo set up video surveillance to catch Toria supposedly in his yard and brought a video over to show Cash. There was a cat in it, but it was impossible to see whether it was Toria or not."

"Okay, thanks Heidi." I looked around for her car. "Do you need a lift?"

"No, I'm walking." She shifted the deli bag to her other hand. "Just grabbing some lunch."

"Where do you work?" I looked around. The area was full of shops of all kinds.

"Just down the street at Flirts." She pointed. "It's a small shop, but we have a lot of cute things."

"Well, enjoy your lunch, and Heidi . . ." I touched her arm.

She paused; impatience washed across her face.

"If you need to talk to someone, just call me. Okay?"

"Okay." She nodded and scurried across the intersection.

An odd exchange.

She'd seemed hurried, but that could just be that she had limited time for lunch. What was most peculiar to me, though, was that while Heidi had asked a lot of questions about my being in Jake and Cash's house, she'd asked nothing about whether I'd heard anything more about Cash's disappearance.

MALONE CALLED and arranged to meet me at Cash and Jake's house. I had one client house call and then I'd meet the detective there and show him the location of the secret room. I'd been to this client's house before, so I knew where I was going. As I cruised up the tree-lined residential street, my mind was still on the conversation I'd just had with Cash's girlfriend.

I shook my head. I needed to rope in my thoughts and concentrate on the upcoming appointment. This particular dog was an interesting case. In my mind I called it "The Case of the Terrible Teacup" because it always made me smile just a little that the tiny teacup poodle was terrorizing both her owner and the neighborhood. But in truth, it wasn't funny at all because if the dog bit again she could be slated for doggie detention and her owner could find herself in hot water and even potential legal troubles.

Audra Collins had adopted Nina as a puppy, and the little poodle still looked like a puppy though she was three years old. She was a chocolate teacup and one of the cutest things I had ever seen. She actually looked like a child's toy she was so tiny and delicate.

When Audra lost her job working for a financial company, the two became best buddies and constant companions. I knew Nina had helped Audra get through a really difficult time.

Audra had taken some online courses to brush up on her skills and recently landed a great job working as an accountant for a local investment group. That's when the trouble started.

When Nina first started misbehaving, Audra would come home to trash all over the house. (Kind of reminds you of Betty's big-dog problems doesn't it?) Nina then moved to tearing up pillows and furniture to where Audra had thought her first few paychecks were going to have to be used to replace her furniture.

But then the situation got worse. Nina became aggressive and had actually nipped at Audra and a neighbor who was outside in his yard.

It was a tough case. Nina had gotten used to Audra being home and hanging out with her, but now Audra needed to help Nina cope with the day-long absences. I had suggested that Audra give Nina some things to do during the times she was gone.

Also I thought Audra could try leaving for shorter periods of time. Because she felt so guilty about leaving her loyal fur-friend who'd gotten her through a terrible time, she was only leaving the toy poodle when she went to work, which signaled to Nina that when Audra left, it was going to be for a long time. I thought if Audra would leave to run some errands and come back in less time, the more frequent coming and going might help Nina to realize that she was not being left behind forever.

My last visit, Audra had agreed to try these tactics, and for this visit I'd planned to check in and see how successful the strategy had been.

I pulled up front and parked. Audra's house was a low bungalow in the village section of Laguna Beach and had a small front porch which had been decorated with colorfully painted chairs and flower pots. I knocked, and as I did I felt a presence beside me.

Audra opened the door just as I turned to face my ex-husband. Where had he come from?

"Caro." Audra's dark-brown hair was pulled back in a ponytail, and her freshly scrubbed face was dotted with freckles. "Please come in." When we'd first met, the girl was shy as a crocus, but this new position seemed to be bringing her out of her shell.

Geoff stepped forward and took her hand. "Hello, I'm Geoffrey Carlisle, and I'm observing Carolina's expertise today. I hope you don't mind."

"Of course not." Audra blushed at the attention. "Please join us."

This was Geoffrey at his best. Charming and attentive.

I couldn't blame Audra for being captivated. I'd once been young and naïve and had fallen for Geoffrey Carlisle's crock of charisma.

It was also typical Geoffrey in that he'd done something totally inappropriate by inserting himself into my client house call, and had done it in such a way that I couldn't put him in his place without coming across like I was the rude one.

"Where is Nina?" I asked as we settled on the couch. A new couch if I wasn't mistaken.

"She's napping in her doggie bed." Audra smiled. "Can you believe it?"

"Well, I was about to ask about progress, but I think the fact she isn't on high alert tells me what I need to know."

Audra opened the door to a side room, and Nina yipped and scurried out. She sniffed Geoff, sniffed me, and then ran to her owner.

"We've just returned from a long walk. Well, long for her anyway," Audra laughed. "So she's tired. I've been walking her a little every day, as you suggested, which has been good for her and for me."

"That's great." I reached over and scratched Nina behind her tiny ears.

Geoff sat quietly observing and listening.

What was the man up to? If he thought taking an interest in what I was doing would win me back, he couldn't be more wrong.

"I've also tried your suggestion of having some noise in the house while I'm gone, such as setting the television timer so the TV is on for a while after I leave, and that seems to help."

"She's beautiful." Geoff smiled at Audra.

Phony. He didn't care for small dogs and when we'd been married had insisted the only dog worth having, if you had to have one, was a big dog. Preferably pure bred.

"Nina started having problems when I went back to work." Audra directed her remarks to Geoff. "She began destroying the house, barking all day, and even became a bit aggressive."

Nina looked at us with dark, innocent eyes as if we must be talking about some other dog. "I would never . . . ," her expression seemed to say.

"What about your neighbor?" I asked. "Any further problems there?"

"No, in fact he stopped over last night and not a yip out of her."

"So the therapy for her separation anxiety appears to have been successful." Geoff propped his chin on his knuckles in a pose I'd seen many times before. "You've done a wonderful job, Audra, in working with her."

"Thank you." She tucked her hair behind one ear and blushed.

Alrighty then. I needed to get him out of there.

"It sounds like you just need to keep doing what you're doing and, please, feel free to give me a call if you run into any problems." I stood.

"I appreciate it, Caro. I can't tell you what a relief it is to not have to worry every day when I come home about what Nina has done this time." She reached over and stroked the little pup's nose.

Geoff slowly rose to his feet. He shook hands with Audra and gave a slight bow. "Thank you so much, Audra, for letting me sit in on Carolina's visit. I hope it wasn't a problem."

"Oh, not at all." She smiled up at him.

We said good-bye and walked to my car. I waited until we were out of earshot.

"What in the Sam Hill do you think you're doing, Geoff?" I saw a bit of a flicker in his deep-blue eyes, but he didn't respond immediately. That was new.

He took a deep breath and rubbed his forehead as if dealing with a difficult thought. "Don't you think you're overreacting, Carolina?"

"Am I?" I bit out.

Unbelievable. He was unbelievable.

"Is it really so awful to want to learn about what you do?"

"If you don't understand what's wrong with showing up uninvited on a business call, then I sure as-shootin' don't know how to explain it to you, Geoff." I stared him down.

"I apologize, my dear." He held up his hands like he was warding off physical blows instead of verbal ones. "I did not know I needed an invitation."

I opened the passenger side door and threw my things in the seat.

"May I come along on your next call?"

"No, you may not." I got in my car before I was tempted to smack him upside the head just to punctuate my sentence.

Thanks to Geoff and his mistaken notion that it was okay to tag along on my house call, I had less than ten minutes to get to Jake and Cash's house to meet Malone. I started the car and looked around, but Geoff was gone.

WHEN I PULLED into the driveway I was again struck by the whimsical nature of the place. Two geeky guys, one adorable cat, and a magical house with a secret room.

Malone's gun-metal-grey Camaro glided into the drive and parked beside me. Precise, powerful, and straightforward like the man behind the wheel.

I got out and waited while Malone finished a cell-phone call and then joined me in front of the house.

My head whipped around when a smaller car also pulled in and parked. It was a white Toyota Prius with a *Channel 5 News* logo on the side, and I suddenly knew who had joined us. I just didn't know how he'd known we were going to be here. Maybe he had a mole at the police station. Or maybe he was the psychic instead of Suzanne.

Reporter Callum MacAvoy got out on the passenger side, and the driver, who apparently doubled as cameraman, followed and then began assembling his camera equipment. In a matter of minutes a tripod was setup and MacAvoy had his TV face on.

"Here we are at the site of Laguna Beach's most recent murder with the detective investigating and the woman who discovered the body."

Malone ignored him and jogged with purpose up the stairs to the front entrance. I followed his lead.

"Ms. Lamont, what are you and the detective doing here? Revisiting the crime scene?" He shoved his wireless microphone toward me and followed me up the steps.

I slipped through the door that Malone held open. MacAvoy attempted to follow, and Malone blocked his access with a muscular arm across the entrance.

"This is still a crime scene." His tone had the ring of authority but didn't deter Mr. TV.

"What are you looking for, Detective?"

Malone didn't answer but instead closed the door in the reporter's face.

"That's okay," MacAvoy yelled through the door. "We'll wait right here."

"How do you think he found out we were going to be here?" I shook my head.

"I don't know. I didn't share my plans with him." Malone's laser blue gaze pinned me.

"You can't think I had anything to do with it." I knew Malone was often frustrated with me and my need to help, but I thought he also knew me well enough to know I didn't seek attention.

"Didn't say you did." He turned away. "But someone had to have leaked it." His body language said there'd be hell to pay when he figured out who.

He looked up the staircase. "This secret room is up there?"

"That's right." I led the way up the stairs and to the turret office.

Stepping into the room, I stopped. There was no gaping wall. No secret room. The open space was now closed up, and you would never know there was anything behind it.

"The opening was right there." I pointed to the wall.

Malone felt along the molding and ran his hands along the floorboard.

"Something here has to open it." I picked up the papers Toria had scattered and stacked them on the desk. There was a wooden inbox, and I dropped the papers in it and straightened the box. As I did, it revealed a button the same color as the ebony desk. It blended in so you might not see it immediately, and the box had been strategically placed to cover it.

"Maybe this." I pointed it out to Malone.

"Push it." He nodded.

The panel slid open just as I remembered.

But all that was behind the door was a wall of empty shelves.

All of the equipment, all of the blinking lights. Gone.

I was speechless.

Malone looked at me, his face serious. "I assume this is not what it looked like earlier today."

I shook my head. I was glad he didn't think I'd lost my mind. I was beginning to doubt my sanity. He seemed to take my word that there truly had been a secret room full of equipment.

"No, there were . . ." I waved my hand toward where all the electronics had been. "And all the boxes were blinking. They kind of looked like some kind of computers, but you know, not like my computer at home."

"Well, it appears someone didn't want us to find whatever was here."

"Who do you think?"

"The obvious answer is Graham Cash."

"Why would he steal stuff from his own home?"

"I don't know. Could be it's something he needs wherever he is. Could be it's something that would incriminate him." He examined the opening, running his hands over the mechanism. Then stepped into the room and stared at the shelves.

"It could be the guy that was here earlier who was hiding in there. I wish I'd been able to get a license number for his car."

"We've asked around to see if anyone in the neighborhood saw him or has seen the car before." Malone wandered the circular room, inventorying everything with his eyes.

"I talked to the guy next door." I pointed out the window at the house. "He was outside when I left but he claimed he didn't see the guy."

"Claimed?" He continued his visual cataloging.

"I don't know how he could have missed him."

"Maybe he was busy or not paying attention or doesn't want to get involved. You'd be surprised how uncooperative eyewitnesses are."

"Heidi, Cash's girlfriend, says the guy had claimed Toria was vicious."

"Toria is the cat?"

"Yes, she's named after Queen Victoria, and I've not seen anything to make me think she'd be aggressive."

"Hmmm." His tone said he wasn't all that interested in how Cash had named his cat or my assessment of Toria's temperament.

"I wonder what that guy was doing here," I mused.

"I'd just as soon you didn't wonder anything." Malone turned to look at me.

"I know. I know."

"And if you hear from Cash again, see if you can find out where he is before he hangs up. And make sure he knows he must call me."

"I feel bad about that, but he really didn't give me a chance to ask anything."

Malone paced the small space. "I'll get our crime-scene techs up here to see if there are fingerprints or anything else that would tell us who has been here, but I'm not very hopeful."

I stared at the empty shelves. Whoever it was had been pretty thorough. "What are we going to do about the persistent press outside?"

"We're going to go out, get in our cars, and drive away."

We made our way back downstairs. Malone phoned in his request for a CSI tech, and I stared out at the patio. The pool area hadn't really been cleaned up. The energy drink I'd knocked over still lay on its side. I remembered the chill of the liquid as it spilled onto my already soaked jeans. I shivered.

When I closed my eyes, I could still see Jake's face when I'd finally been able to turn him over. How on earth did people manage to go on living in a house when there had been a violent crime? I wondered who would clean up the place with Jake dead and Cash missing. Were there relatives? Neither of them had talked that much about their personal lives.

I knew Malone was convinced Cash was involved, if not actually Jake's killer, but I hoped and prayed he wasn't.

Granted, it looked darn suspicious that he'd disappeared at the same time. But though he'd sounded furtive on the phone, he hadn't sounded like someone on the run. Whatever that sounded like.

Besides if it were him, what was the motive? The two were successful partners and from what I could tell had always seemed to get along.

And besides, if Cash were on the run, he would have taken his cat. The man was truly attached to his cat.

Detective Malone, or Detective Hottie as Betty liked to call him, finished up his call and glanced my way.

"You okay?"

"I'm fine."

He walked to the entry and peered out. "Still there. All right, we're going to out. You go first and I'll follow a little slower. He'll go for me and you should be able to get in your car and drive away. Ready?"

"Ready." I nodded.

Malone opened the door, and I stepped through. The reporter pounced right away. I made a beeline for my car as Malone had instructed. Malone lagged behind, and I could see the dilemma on Mr. TV's face.

He turned toward Malone. "Detective, what did you find?" Obviously an official comment would carry more air-time clout.

"No comment," I could hear Malone answer.

I reached my car, opened the door, and looked his way.

Malone gave a slight nod, and I slid in and started my car.

I drove quickly to the next house call which was a couple with a young Bichon Frisé. Bichon Frisé means "curly lap dog," and Alf was that and so much more. The dogs are small and sturdy, and their dark inquisitive eyes are guaranteed to tug at your heartstrings.

Judi and Michael, the couple who owned Alf, had been referred to me by Dr. Daniel Darling, a good friend and our local veterinarian. Alf had developed such a severe limp they could no longer take him for walks. Dr. Daniel, after a full battery of tests, had ruled out any possible injury or physical cause for the limp. He recommended they have me take a look at Alf and get my thoughts.

This was just a get-to-know-you visit. As you might have already figured out, much of my work with problem pets is really working with pet parents. To truly assess the situation, I've got to understand the day-to-day workings of the household and the people dynamics as well as the pet ones.

The little dog was friendly but would sometimes whine as if hurt. Often, the couple said, it happened if Alf were touched unexpectedly. His limp was pronounced, but he was still playful and chased down toys or treats. I enjoyed the time with the couple and with Alf and had some ideas but held back on sharing them. I wanted to do a little research first on post-traumatic stress in animals. I promised to drop back by in a week.

Relieved the couple hadn't questioned me about seeing me on the news or the murder investigation, I stopped by the office and in the quiet transcribed a few of my notes. I'd intended to only do some preliminary research on the topic of PTSD in animals, but when I finally glanced at the clock, I realized I'd been at it almost an hour. It was surprising, both on the human side and the animal side, how little we understood about the effect of traumatic events on the psyche. Puppy mill dogs often show varying degrees of post-traumatic stress disorder due to the abhorrent conditions they've endured. I knew Judi and Mark would never buy from a puppy mill, but they'd gotten Alf from a friend, so the transfer of ownership was unclear.

If I was right, it would take patience and dedication to rehabilitate Alf, and so I wanted to be sure before I offered an opinion.

I stopped outside my office door to make sure I had my car keys. Psychic Suzanne stepped into the lobby from her office at the same time. It looked like she was calling it a day as well.

"Have a good evening," I called to her.

"Beware of strangers," she replied as she walked out.

I closed my door with an irritated snap. The woman had a knack for throwing out unsettling but generic warnings.

Starting my car, I tuned the radio to a favorite classical station and was pleased when the strains of Mozart's Eine kleine Nachtmusik began. I put the car in gear. A little night music was exactly what I needed as I slowly drove home to my pets and what I hoped was a quiet evening.

What a day.

I could not believe all the equipment that had been in the hidden room had just disappeared. It begged the question: who else knew about the room? Heidi hadn't, and she was close to Cash. So, who else could have come into a locked house and carted away all those electronic things between the time I'd left and Malone and I had come back?

I wondered if Malone had had any luck with the crime-scene team. I hadn't heard from him. Not that I'm saying the man has to check in with me, but he had to know I was curious.

It wasn't late, but the evening seemed darker than usual, overcast and quiet. A sliver of moonlight reached out from behind the clouds but didn't make much of a dent in the darkness. I pulled into my drive, hit the garage-door opener button, pulled in, and hit the closer. As the door slid down I noticed a man across the street. I glanced around for the dark SUV I'd been seeing. Nothing in sight.

Grabbing my things, I got out of the car and went in. Once inside I dropped my bag and kicked off my shoes. I felt a little spooked and wished I'd gotten a better look, but I wasn't going back outside. My next-door neighbor April Mae was traveling with her painting cats. (Long story but the cats really do paint, and people buy their paintings.) Freda, my neighbor on the other side was gone on an Alaskan cruise. I reminded myself I needed to get over to her house and check on her plants.

I walked through the house and greeted the animals, but the prickle of uneasiness I'd felt didn't leave me. I don't spook easily, but I guess having found a dead guy, a secret room, and a mysterious intruder, all in two days' time, kind of had me on edge.

I fished my cell phone out of my bag and kept it handy just in case.

Just in case of what, I wasn't sure. I didn't immediately turn on any lights but peered out the living-room window which faced the front of the house. I couldn't see anyone anymore.

Wait. Was that someone moving in the shadows near the neighbor's Manzanita tree? I stared hard at the darkness.

No, it was just a branch.

I flipped on the kitchen light and laid my cell phone on the counter. Opening the refrigerator, I perused my options for dinner. I definitely needed to do a Whole Foods run. I should have stopped by before coming home, but my mind had been on other things. Murder will do that.

I pulled eggs, spinach, mushrooms, and goat cheese from the fridge. Okay, an omelet it was. I promised myself I'd do serious shopping tomorrow. Tonight I was simply too beat to deal with going back out for groceries.

My kitchen was small but efficient. I reach in a lower cabinet for a pan and set it on the stove. As I started to turn on the burner, my doorbell rang. I set the pan aside and went to answer the door.

I know what you're thinking. And no, I didn't just fling open the door without looking. I'm not like one of those too-dumb-to-live heroines in the low-budget horror movies, oblivious to the danger and inviting in the axe murderer.

I'd picked up my cell phone, 911 at the ready, and looked out the front window again. I couldn't see anything.

I walked to my entryway and leaned against the door. "Who is it?"

"Your favorite reporter," came the reply in that distinctive broadcast voice. "Callum MacAvoy."

Well for cryin' in a bucket! I understood persistence was important in his field, but Callum MacAvoy was headed right to number one on my never-want-to-see-you-again list.

I yanked open the door. "How did you get my address?"

"I'm an investigative reporter; you're on damn near every civic committee in town; it wasn't difficult." He rolled his eyes. "Listen, I just have a few questions for you." His dark chinos and the white shirt with a *Channel 5 News* logo on the pocket made it seem like he was here in an official capacity.

I peered behind him. I didn't see a cameraperson with him.

"You know what, Mr. MacAvoy?"

"My friends call me 'Mac,'" he corrected. "Can I come in?"

"We're not friends and no, you can't come in." I braced my foot against the door ready to slam it shut if need be. "I appreciate that you're a reporter and it's your job to report, but I've got nothing for you."

"But you and the homicide detective were doing something at the Internet tycoons' house."

"Not really." Yes we were, but I sure wasn't going to share what that was, and I couldn't bring myself to outright lie.

"What kind of cat is that?" From his vantage point he had a view of my entryway.

Toria had come to see what the excitement was and meowed in greeting. She was such a calm and serene cat. I could only hope some of her sweetness rubbed off on Thelma and Louise.

"It's a Scottish Fold tabby." Toria leaned against my ankles rubbing her head on my shoes.

"How long have you had her?" I knew what he was doing. He was trying to keep me talking, lulling me into being chatty, hoping I'd reveal something. No deal.

"Not long." I stepped outside so there wasn't any danger of Toria slipping out. I knew he'd deliberately left an opening, but I was not going to share that she was Graham Cash's cat.

"I've never seen a cat that fat. Are all tabby cats that big?"

"Tabby isn't a breed. It describes the markings." I was deliberately short with him.

"Then what's a—what did you call it—Scottish Fold?" he asked.

"All Scottish Fold cats today can trace their heritage back to Susie, a white mouser with unusual folded ears, who lived in Scotland's Tayside region. A man who got one of Susie's kittens, Snooks, started the whole lineage, and soon breeders became involved and discovered the folded ears was a dominant trait."

"Dominant trait? What does that mean?" He tipped his head like

Dogbert does when he's trying to understand a point I'm making.

"It means if one parent has the gene for straight ears and the other parent folded ears, their offspring would have folded ears." I stopped. Dang it, he had got me talking. "Were you planning to do a special feature on cat breeds?"

"Nope." He smiled a big on-camera smile. "Still interested in talking to you about the murder."

"Still got nothing to tell you."

"Are you a person of interest?" He didn't have a microphone, but if he had, it would have been jammed in my face at this point.

"No, I am not."

"Do you know if they have a person of interest?"

"I don't," I sighed, "and Mr. MacAvoy, if I knew I wouldn't tell you."

He was undeterred. "I know from the scuttlebutt that you were the one to find the murder victim. What can you tell me about the crime scene?"

"I thought you were the noon reporter. I'm sure I saw you do the report on the Laguna Women's Club Craft Bazaar." Maybe if I insulted him he'd go away.

MacAvoy rolled his eyes. "For now, but when something opens up on the news team I'll be moving to prime time."

"Uh, huh." He hoped.

"What's the deal with you and your cousin?"

"Long story and not a very interesting one." I turned to go back inside. "And none of your business," I added over my shoulder.

"I just wondered. You know, since she's not engaged anymore."

"What?" Without thinking, I turned and grabbed the front of his shirt. "What did you say?"

"I said she's not engaged anymore to that creepy guy, Grey Donovan. I told her something wasn't right with him."

"You told her what?" It seemed now I was the one asking the questions. I let go of his shirtfront.

"Yeah, all that stuff with the Dachshund races and criminals. He knew a lot more than he was letting on."

Mel's fiancé, Grey Donovan, was not creepy by any stretch of the imagination. He was a prince of a guy, and yes, I knew he had secrets. I didn't pry, but I knew he was more than just a successful art dealer. I figured some sort of undercover work, but whatever it was, he had chosen not to share, and I respected that. He and Melinda had been off and on before, so I hoped this was just a tiff that would blow over. Betty hadn't said anything, so maybe Mr. Not-Ready-for-Prime-Time had his facts wrong.

"Again, none of your business."

"Okay, okay." He held up a hand. "Don't get all huffy with me."

"I've had a long day, Mr. MacAvoy. And I'm hungry. We're done."

"Fine. If you think of anything here's my card." He held out a business card, but I didn't reach for it, and he finally dropped his hand.

"I understand the victim had some problems with the next-door neighbor."

"Who told you that?" I'd thought it was Cash not Jake. Did he know something I didn't or was he simply baiting me?

"Let's see. I think the first to tell me was Heidi Sussman, Graham Cash's girlfriend. Though I'm not sure they were exclusive."

Heidi had mentioned the problem between Cash and the neighbor related to Toria, but nothing about Jake. Though I guess she'd been in a hurry to get back to work, and there hadn't been any reason to share anything further with me. I had to think when Malone had interviewed her she'd have told him.

"Wait, what did you say?"

"I said, Jake, the dead guy had some issues with the next-door neighbor."

"No, the part about they weren't exclusive."

"Some of the people I've talked to said Heidi Sussman had made a play for Jake before she hooked up with his business partner."

"Some people?"

"You know, friends. I've talked to some of their local friends in the course of my investigative reporting."

"You mean snooping?" I knew an accusatory tone had slipped into my voice, but I couldn't help it. Like I said before, reporters and I have a history. Especially those who report on other people's trouble.

"Come on, Caro. Cut me some slack." He rubbed a hand over his face and dropped his on-air voice. "I'm just trying to do my job here."

I supposed he was right. The guy was just seeking information about Jake's murder and the investigation surrounding it. I knew I was hyper-sensitive about reporters because during the course of my rather messy divorce, I'd become the target of some sensationalized reporting of every lurid detail. It was bad enough to watch your marriage and your career crash and burn, but it made it even worse if you couldn't go anywhere without whispers and side-looks because everyone knew all the intimate details.

"According to these friends I talked to, Jake and Cash had a party at the house with a pretty big crowd in attendance and this neighbor claimed his fence was damaged. There was a big shouting match between him and Jake." MacAvoy watched my face, waiting for my reaction.

Mr. TV's tactics were obvious. I hadn't responded to flattery, or to the lure of camera time, but he'd found my currency. I wanted information he had, and he was trying to figure out what I was willing to trade.

"I really don't have anything for you, Mr. MacAvoy." I rested my hand on the doorknob. "I'd suggest you talk to Detective Malone."

"Thank you for your time." He held out the card again, and this time I took it. "And good luck with the weird-looking cat." He waved as he walked away, and I opened the door and went back inside.

What on earth? I dropped my cell phone on the counter and went back to my omelet.

Melinda and Grey no longer engaged?
Heidi playing both Jake and Cash?
Jake in a heated exchange with the odd neighbor?

It seemed strange Heidi hadn't mentioned the fight between Jake and the neighbor, but depending on when it happened maybe she wasn't aware of it. Heidi making a play for Jake and then landing on Cash wasn't too surprising and whether fair-play rules were violated depended on when she changed her mind. As far as my cousin, Mel, I was shocked Betty hadn't mentioned Mel and Grey's breakup if it really were true.

Or it could be Mr. TV just enjoyed stirring the pot.

Chapter Seven

THE SMELL OF disinfectant, and of dogs, cats, and other furry friends, was comfortingly normal. It was my day to volunteer at the Laguna Beach Animal Rescue League shelter. I routinely helped out at the ARL a few hours once a week, working with any problem animals in order to catch issues that might keep them from being adopted. If there were no problem pets, I exercised dogs, played with kittens, or cleaned cages. It was the best therapy in the world.

Don Furry was a good guy and a regular volunteer at the Animal Rescue. He was sorting through supplies in the storage area when I arrived. A little past middle-aged, Don worked circles around others half his age. He was a stalwart rescue supporter, and I frankly didn't know what the shelter would do without him.

"Good morning, Don."

"Hello, Caro." He stopped sorting and turned to look at me. "How are you?"

It wasn't just the cursory how-are-you greeting; I could tell from the way his eyes searched my face, it was real concern. Without a doubt, he'd also seen the news report.

"I am doing okay," I answered.

"The television account said you found the young man who drowned." He squatted down to stack bags of donated litter on a lower shelf.

"That's right." I stepped into the storage room and handed him another bag from the pile on the floor. "Jake was one of the partners in the computer company that has space in our office."

"That had to be rough." Don glanced up.

"It was," I answered. "And Cash, the other partner, is missing."

"I didn't catch that part on the news." He finished with the cat litter shelf and stood. "Though come of think of it, when they showed the clip, you were holding a small animal carrier."

"I have Toria, Graham Cash's Scottish Fold cat," I explained.

"Those are cute cats." He stood and dusted off his hands on his jeans. "Glad you were able to take her because we are full up."

That was unfortunately not unusual at our shelter and many others. Too few people, too little funding, and too many animals. Don moved on to the paper goods and began unbundling a shrink-wrapped pallet of paper towels.

"What do you have for me, Don?" I stowed my things and pulled my still slightly damp red curls into a hair band I'd brought along. Jeans and a well-worn PUPS (Protecting Unwanted Pets) T-shirt were standard attire for my volunteer days, and there was no point in trying to tame my hair. It would be a lost cause with the workout a few hours at the shelter presented.

"Not much. We got a couple of pups who were dumped out in the canyon. Little guys were pretty traumatized, but they seem to be adjusting. Dr. Daniel has looked them over, and there are no injuries. They were mostly just dirty and hungry."

"Idiots." Nothing got me wound up faster than people who thought it was okay to just discard animals. "They could have brought them to us."

"Lucky for them we're going through a dry spell." He bounced a ball into the storage bin. "The gully they were in fills with water when it rains hard."

"I'll take a peek at them and then help Chelley with the cages."

"She's tied up right now talking to a customer who wants to adopt."

"That's great." Before heading back to look at the pups, I went through to the front desk to let Chelley know I was there. Big-boned, boisterous, and all heart, Chelley was a favorite with the other volunteers and with customers. Her bottle-blond hair pulled back in a ponytail, she was also attired in jeans and a PUPS T-shirt. She generally kept the administrative side of things running, but like Don, she also pitched in wherever she was needed. A man stood at the desk with her.

"Hey, Chelley, I hear we have some new residents."

"Hi, Caro." She looked up with a broad smile. "I'll be there in just a few minutes. This gentleman is looking to adopt a dog."

The customer looked familiar. I tried to place him. Where did I know him from? Then it came to me: he was the man who'd had car trouble the other day and had used the phone at the office.

"Hi, there." I laid my hand on his arm. "Did you get your car trouble taken care of?"

He jumped and shook my hand off.

"Oh, I'm sorry." I hadn't meant to startle him. "You probably don't remember me."

He continued to stare at me. Apparently I wasn't too memorable. Or maybe the pulled-back hair didn't help.

"I'm Caro, the pet therapist," I reminded him. "You used the phone at our office a couple of days ago."

"Oh, right, right," he stuttered. "You work here, too?"

"I volunteer at least once a week. Our shelter, like many others, is underfunded and understaffed, so we rely on volunteers to fill the gap."

"Thank you for your time," he said to Chelley. "I appreciate it."

"Did you find a dog you're interested in?" I asked.

"Mr. Kemper is interested in a basset hound," she explained. "And currently we don't have any bassets in our ready-to-adopt group."

"Ah." Sometimes, but not always, people came in with a particular breed in mind.

"You might think about the black Lab if you have the space," Chelley encouraged. "Even though Pharaoh is a little bigger dog, Labs are very social like basset hounds. And he's a sweetheart."

"Thank you, ma'am." He glanced toward the cages. "I'll think about it. I really like the basset hound."

Once the man was gone, Chelley showed me the puppies. After they were cleared by Dr. Daniel, spayed and neutered, and given a clean bill of health, they would be available for adoption. Puppies are adopted much more quickly than adult dogs, so I didn't imagine they'd be around long. After a few minutes for cuddles and snuggles, we rolled up our sleeves and began the task of cleaning out the cages. The big dogs had already been done so we concentrated on the smaller dogs, cats, and bunnies.

"Did you know the guy who was here looking for a basset hound?" she asked.

"He'd had car trouble near my office a few days ago and borrowed the phone to call his auto club, but I'd not met him before that."

"I didn't want to push, but I never understand it when people get hung up on a certain breed. The Lab would be a great dog for him."

"Pharaoh is a great dog and will make someone a wonderful companion." I glanced over at Chelley. "Maybe he's just not the right match for—" I paused. "I'm sorry what was the man's name?"

"Wayne," she answered. "Wayne Kemper. He has his own hedge-trimming and tree service, 'The Cutting Hedge.'"

We snickered at the name. The man sure hadn't seemed like he had much of a sense of humor, but the business name was clever. Maybe he just took a while to warm up to people.

"Do we have a basset hound?" I thought I'd seen one come in.

We do our cat enclosure cleaning leaving the cats in place, and so it didn't take us long to finish that area. We moved on to the visiting rooms.

"Yes, but we're still holding him in hopes his owner will come for him." Chelley wiped down the walls making short work of the first room. "He was hungry and tired when City Animal Control found him but didn't look like he'd been out in the elements very long. We've posted information both online and in local stores because the dog looked well cared for. But so far no owners have shown up."

"That's too bad. No microchip?" I followed behind her, finishing the walls with a clean rinse.

"Unfortunately, no, he didn't have a chip."

The biggest problem we had with lost pets was tracing their owners. Sadly, only about fifteen to twenty percent are reunited with their families. But thankfully more and more pets now are microchipped. This is where a little device is inserted just under their skin. The chips are very small, but each has a unique number that can be read by a scanner and matched with owner information. Our veterinarian makes sure each animal we adopt out has the identifying chip, and we make sure the new pet parents are registered.

Once Chelley and I were done with the visiting rooms, I went to say good-bye to Don Furry. He was exercising a couple of the bigger dogs in the large workout room we'd set up, throwing tennis balls for them to chase down.

"I'll stop by in the next couple of days and take Pharaoh to the dog park for a run if you like. Chelley doesn't think he's getting enough fresh air and exercise."

"That would be a great idea. I try to get them out when I can, but this week we're short-handed so I'd sure appreciate the help." He took the ball Pharaoh had brought back to him and threw it again. The happy Lab chased after it racing the length of the canine corral.

"No problem. I'll see you later then." I waved good-bye and went to pick up my things. I planned to stop back by my house to change out of my cage-cleaning clothes.

As I walked to my car, I checked my phone and happily noted I had a voice mail from my friend Diana. Hopefully we could set a lunch date.

After I saw the story about Jake's murder on the news, I'd called and left her a message that I was okay, but I was looking forward to chatting with her in person. Diana always helped put things in perspective for me. I had no idea how old Diana was, not that it mattered, but she'd been the perky star of many romantic comedies a few decades ago. Though retired from the silver screen, she hadn't lost her classic beauty or her feisty personality. We'd met as volunteers at the ARL, worked on a couple of rescue fundraisers together, and, united by our love of fashion and pets, had become fast friends.

I listened to her voice mail message. She asked me to call her back, but she also mentioned she'd sprained her ankle. I dialed her number before getting in my car.

"My word, Diana, what did you do?" I settled into the car seat but left the door open.

"It's nothing serious, just a nuisance." I noted she hadn't really answered my question about how she'd injured herself. "I wondered, if it wouldn't be too much trouble, if you could help me out with a couple of things?"

"I'd love to. What can I do?" Without a doubt Diana was doing more than she was supposed to be. Like the dog park, the shelter was on Laguna Canyon Road, and I watched cars buzz by on the busy roadway as I listened. There'd been no sign of being followed today, and I was, in this case, pleased to be wrong.

"I had a special necklace made at Baubles, that new shop downtown, and they've called to say it's ready." I was sure a special order for Diana was a really extraordinary creation. "I wouldn't rush to pick it up, but they're going to be closed for a few days, so if I don't get it today, it will be a while."

"Super. I haven't been in there yet." I swung my legs in and shut the car door. "It'll give me a chance to look around." And seeing Diana would allow me an opportunity to get her take on all that had transpired the last couple of days.

"Oh, thank you." I could hear barking in the background which was the usual ambient noise at Diana's. "And"—she hesitated—"I hate to ask for another favor, but Bella's got her hands full with me and the crew."

"Ask away." It had to be driving her crazy to not be able to operate at her usual jack-rabbit pace.

"I have some boxes of supplies that need to be dropped off at the shelter."

"No problem, sugar," I assured her. I didn't tell her I was at the shelter already or she'd fuss about a second trip. "I am happy to do it."

"Thanks so much, Caro." There was a sharp bark, and she shushed Mr. Wiggles, her puggle, who I pictured sitting on her lap. "And if you can come by around noon, you must plan to stay for lunch."

"You've got it. But only if you promise not go to any trouble." It took very little to twist my arm about lunch, but I thought the whole purpose of my running the errands was so that she could be resting her ankle. "In fact, why don't I bring lunch?"

"No, I've already got it covered," she insisted. I could picture her wide smile. "See you soon."

Starting my car, I felt myself relax as I turned onto the roadway and drove back toward town. It wouldn't take me but a few minutes to stop by home, grab a quick shower, and change clothes before picking up Diana's necklace. I looked forward to visiting the new shop, and even more I loved the idea of lunch and a chat.

A dose of Diana Knight was just what I needed.

Chapter Eight

BAUBLES, THE SHOP where I was to pick up Diana's necklace, was just off of Pacific Coast Highway, PCH to the locals, and nestled between a row of art galleries. What a great location for both local customers and tourists, and the cases and shelves of the new shop were packed with one-of-a-kind pieces.

As I waited for Neeley, the designer and proprietor, to locate Diana's special order, I walked around the shop. The walls were painted a soothing taupe, and the windows were unadorned to let in plenty of daylight. The jewelry and other trinkets were all made with natural stones and gems. I was drawn to an ocean-themed display in the back and went for a closer look.

I'd knelt down to look at a shell-shaped paperweight made from some sort of white stone when the bell on the door dinged, signaling a new customer. Heidi Sussman walked in with another girl I didn't recognize. I could see them clearly from my place on the floor, but they didn't notice me.

"I'll be right with you," Neeley called out from the back.

The two girls continued their conversation. They were dressed in yoga pants and crop tops. Heidi in her signature pink and the other girl in vivid purple.

"Morgan, look at this." Heidi stretched out a strong tanned arm and held up a sparkly strand of pink stones. Pink topaz or tourmaline would be my guess. It was too clear for quartz.

"Oh, that's so you." The other girl giggled.

"It is, isn't it." Heidi draped it against her chest.

They moved on to another case with rings, bracelets, and hair accessories. "So what do the police think happened with Jake?" the girl Heidi had called Morgan asked in a low voice.

"They aren't telling me." Heidi flipped a blond lock over her shoulder and reached for a mirror that sat on the counter top. She slipped off a hair clip she wore and tried on a sparkling headband encrusted with stones.

"Do you think it had anything to do with the argument they got into at Mozambique last Friday?"

"Who knows?" Heidi didn't sound all that interested.

"What do you think Jake was going to tell everyone about Cash?" The other girl picked up a shiny bracelet and slid it onto her wrist.

"I dunno. Something about his past maybe." Heidi put the headband back on the counter and reached for a trio of stack rings.

"Must have been something big. I've never seen Cash lose it like that. He's always so calm. So stiff-upper-lip British."

"I guess." Heidi didn't sound too concerned about the disagreement, but I still couldn't believe she hadn't mentioned the fight before.

Had I been had? On the phone, Cash had sounded like maybe he was in trouble, but how well did I know him? Was it possible he was really the killer? Had he killed Jake to keep him from revealing a secret? Just because he was a great cat dad didn't mean the guy didn't have other problems.

The two girls had moved to the other side of the store.

I stood just as Neeley came from the back with a box.

"Here we go, Caro." She slid the box on the counter. "Did Diana tell you what she ordered?"

"No," I answered. "I know she was really excited about it."

"The piece is an exquisite pearl, citrine, green amethyst, and white topaz necklace. I had so much fun making it."

I could see out of the corner of my eye, Heidi and her friend had spotted me.

"Hello, Caro," she said quietly. She looked uncomfortable, and I guessed she might be wondering just how much I'd heard.

"Would you like to take a look?" I motioned Heidi and her friend over.

"Sure," the friend answered.

The two leaned in beside me as Neeley lifted the necklace from where it nested in the velvet box.

"Wow, Caro. Is it for you?" Heidi asked.

"No, I'm picking it up for a friend," I answered.

"It's so beautiful." Morgan reached out and touched the stones which were attached to the delicate chain in a waterfall fashion. The stones made a tinkling sound as she ran her finger along them.

It was a stunning piece of jewelry and uniquely perfect for Diana Knight.

Neeley gently wrapped the necklace, placed it back in the box, and handed it to me. "Diana has already settled up with me and so you're good to go. Tell her I hope she enjoys it."

She turned to the two girls. "Can I help you ladies with anything?"

"We were just killing time before our hot yoga class starts," Morgan admitted.

"You have some really pretty things," Heidi added.

"I'm sure Diana will be pleased with her necklace." I smiled at Neeley. "And I'll be back to look at some of the rest of your collections."

The two exited the store with me. As we stepped out into the sunshine, we all three reached for our sunglasses.

"Heidi." I stopped her with a hand on her arm. "What's this about an argument Jake and Cash had?"

"It was no big deal." She shrugged my hand loose. "Don't make it into one." She walked away.

Heidi and Morgan hopped in Heidi's Escalade which was parked at the curb and took off. I watched them pull away, bothered by how dismissive Heidi had been of the disagreement. Was she protecting Cash? What was the secret? And most importantly, had he been angry enough to strangle his friend and partner?

Maybe she was right and it wasn't a big deal. Friends disagree. But one friend was dead, and the other was missing. And the missing one was someone she supposedly cared for. Wouldn't you think she'd be sharing everything, big deal or not, with the police?

I had started walking in the other direction up the street to where my car was parked when Neeley came rushing out of her shop.

"Oh no." She stopped. "Caro, do you know those girls?"

"I know one of them."

"They left this on the counter." She held up a sparkly hair clip.

It was Heidi's. The one she'd taken off to try the headband on. She must have forgotten to pick it up and put it back on.

"Oh, that's Heidi's. I'll return it to her, if you like."

"Would you?" Neeley handed the hair clip to me. "I'd really appreciate it if you could. I'm off to a jewelry show and am closing the shop for a couple of days."

"No problem." It would give me another chance to talk to Heidi and to see if I could find out more information about this argument between Jake and Cash. And maybe I could find out what she knew about Jake's fight with the next-door neighbor that Callum MacAvoy had mentioned.

DIANA KNIGHT lived in Ruby Point, an exclusive gated community just off of PCH. Top-notch security, gorgeous homes, and to-die-for views.

The guard checked me through, and I followed the winding street to Diana's. Pulling my sporty silver car into the flower-lined driveway, I glanced up at the house. It was one of the larger ones on the street and, though not that old, had an old world feel. The front was lush with flower beds filled with elegant roses and feathery lavender. As I got out, I stretched and inhaled the fragrant combination.

Bella, her housekeeper and companion, answered the door surrounded by a few of the members of what I fondly refer to as Diana's zoo.

"Please, come in." The dark-haired Bella's lilting voice was a bit breathless, and she angled her small body to block the doorway, making sure no one escaped. "She is so looking forward to your visit."

Diana had a blended family of rescues: a gorgeous Maine Coon cat, Gypsy; Mr. Wiggles, her lop-eared puggle; Barbary, her grumpy one-eyed basset hound; and Abe, her goat. At one point, there'd also been a rooster, Walter. From time to time there were also foster animals, the difficult-to-adopt ones, who stayed with Diana until forever homes could be found. Sometimes the lucky fosters became permanent members of the household.

I slipped through the door quickly. "How is she doing?"

"*Bien*, good, but she is bored. And impossible to keep down." Bella lifted her hands in a gesture of helplessness. "Thank you for coming."

Diana was in her sunny-yellow kitchen which was state of the art. She'd laid out a sumptuous lunch and was in the process of carrying the food out to the terrace. Her foot was wrapped, and she limped a little, but it didn't seem to be slowing her down much.

"Caro, lovely as always." Diana put down the platter to hug me. Then she kissed my cheek and looked me over head to toe. "Stella McCartney always looks good on you."

She'd nailed it as usual. I'd worn a sleeveless silk paisley crepe-de-chine dress with a racer back. I loved the comfort and the classic lines as well as the softness of the crepe. The dark-blue and deep-burgundy contrasting colors gave it a casual feel.

"You're the one who's good." I swear the woman could pick out most any designer at sixty paces. I had the ones I liked (and some that left me cold), but this lady was a clothes horse of the first order.

I glanced at the spread on the counter top. Sandwiches, mini-salads, fresh fruit, and arranged with an artistic eye. It looked almost too good to eat. Almost.

"What is this?" I chided her. "You shouldn't have gone to so much trouble."

"Oh, pshaw. I know it looks like I've prepared a feast, but I haven't. Bella picked it up for me at Sapphire's Pantry. I just dished it up so it looks fancy." Her trademark impish smile flashed my way as she loaded up her hands.

"Let me get those." I reached for the plates.

"You can grab the iced tea." She nodded toward the pitcher and glasses.

There was a slight ocean kissed breeze. The large terrace was shaded by the palm trees that bordered the property, so the temperature was ideal for outdoor dining. The landscaping had been configured to continue the old-world feel with more blooms and greenery. An occasional glint of the sun on the vast Pacific peeked between the shrubberies and trees, reminding me of its closeness.

Diana was dressed in black-and-white-striped crop pants and a white cotton pullover, but somehow she still managed to look classy. Even with her right ankle wrapped in an elastic bandage. My guess was Diane von Furstenberg (the outfit not the bandage), but I wasn't as accurate as my friend was so I didn't share my speculation aloud.

"So." Diana leaned forward in her chair and took a dainty sip of tea. "What's the latest on the murder?"

"Funny you should ask." I reached for a sandwich. "It seems like new developments at every turn."

I filled her in on the conversation I'd just overheard between Heidi and her friend about the fight Jake and Cash had just a few days prior to Jake's murder.

"It does sound like she should have reported that to the police." Diana moved back and propped her injured foot on a small stool Bella had carried out to the terrace.

"It makes me feel like an idiot for trusting Cash. From the way he sounded on the phone, I truly believed he was in trouble himself." I took a bite of the sandwich, chicken salad with bits of apple and walnut.

"Hon, you're a great judge of character. This disagreement with his partner doesn't mean he lied to you or that he's not in trouble."

"I don't know about the great-judge-of-people pronouncement," I reflected, picking up my glass of tea. "I can think of a case where I really missed the mark."

Diana knew all about my family history and my ugly divorce. I re-counted the bizarre scenario of Geoff showing up at house and then at my appointment.

As I described the scene with Geoff, Sam, and Malone, I could tell she was entertained by the picture I painted. In retrospect it was a little funny in an awkward sort of way, but entertainment I didn't want to repeat any time soon.

"Now, about this Heidi." Diana was back to the murder. "What do you know about Cash's girlfriend?"

"I don't know her well at all. She works at a boutique downtown near Mel's shop. She had stopped in the office occasionally to see Cash, but not very often. She doesn't seem as upset by the fact that he's missing. Or at least not as upset as you'd think she would be."

"And the rude neighbor? Do you know his name?" She leaned back in her chair.

"Hmmm." I took a sip of sweet tea. "I don't think anyone has men-tioned it. Heidi's the one who told me about him and the fuss over his claim of Cash's cat being vicious."

"Well, he seems like a jerk." Diana calls them like she sees them.

I have to say the man did not make a very good impression on me. But then people like Diana (and me) don't cotton much to folks who don't like animals, and he was downright nasty about Toria.

As if she were reading my thoughts, Diana asked. "What about the young man's kitty? I'm sure Toria was falsely accused."

I couldn't believe it had taken her this long to ask about the cat. With Diana it's always about the animals.

"Oh my, Diana, she is flat adorable. I may not give her back. She's about this tall and this wide." I held up my hands to show her. "She's adapted fine to Dogbert and my two felines. Toria is much more of a lap cat than Thelma or Louise, and I think Dogbert is a bit put out about the situation."

"The Scottish Fold cats are so cute. Almost teddy bear-like faces, aren't they?" She began gathering dishes. "What color is she?"

"She's a grey tabby. I gather from what Cash said, he brought her with him from his home in England. He's very attached to her, which is why I can't imagine him taking off and leaving her behind."

"Except he knew he left her in good hands." She looked thoughtful.

"Stop, now. Let me pick up." I took the dishes from her hands.

"If you take those inside, I'll get the rest." She collected the remain-ing items on the table. "I have another favor to ask of you, if you don't mind running one more errand for me."

"Happy to do it." I carried the dishes to the kitchen and went back for the other things.

Diana was on her way inside with more of the remnants of our lunch. I took the tray from her.

"Do you need something else picked up? I enjoyed my side trip to Baubles, and I'm ready and willing for more shopping errands."

"No, in this case, dropped off." She limped inside. "The Laguna Beach Public Library has asked if I'd donate something for their Golden Age of Hollywood exhibit, and though it makes me feel ancient, Bella and I went through my things and found a few items."

"Sounds like fun."

"I'm donating a dress I wore in a movie eons ago and a book about the making of the movie. The author and the costume designer had already signed it, and so I signed it too. I don't know if that will help, but they're welcome to it."

"No problem." I stacked dishes in the sink. "Do I drop the things off at the library?"

"No, to Mary Jo, the woman who's curating everything for the exhibit. Bella has her address and phone number."

"Sounds like an exhibit I'll have to see."

"Oh, and there are the boxes for the ARL that I mentioned before." She grinned, her blue eyes dancing. "You're going to be sorry you offered to help."

"Never." My eyes skimmed her face. I hoped she really was as okay as she claimed.

"It's just a few things I'd picked up for the shelter. I'd intended to drop them off last week, but then that's when I did this." She pointed at her foot in irritation.

"Sugar, I know you're out of patience with it." I hugged her. "You do what the doctor says, and it will be healed before you know it. A silly old sprain can't keep a good woman down."

"That's right." She grinned.

We walked through the kitchen to her living room and got her settled in an easy chair.

"I can't begin to tell you how much I appreciate your help." Diana settled her injured ankle on an ottoman. "There's a basket of cranberry muffins on the counter for you. I tried a new recipe, but it made far too many for Bella and me. Consider it down payment for all of this work I'm causing you."

"I'll check in on you again in a couple of days." I picked up my bag and kissed her on the cheek. "You make me a list."

Bella helped me cart the boxes to my car, her strong brown arms helping me make short work of loading up.

"How is she really doing?" I asked as we packed the items in my trunk.

"Very impatient." She shook her head. "She is supposed to keep her ankle *elevate*, you know, up, to help with the swelling, but she will not stop long enough to do as the doctor said she must. I am afraid she's going to make it worse."

"How did she do it?" I asked. "She wouldn't tell me."

"Her pride." Bella smiled, her dark eyes dancing. "And she didn't want you to worry. She was getting down from her trampoline." She handed me another box. "No, no. I see what you are thinking. Not that kind."

She could apparently tell from the expression on my face that I was picturing elegant Diana bouncing up and down on a trampoline.

"It is one of those little ones she jogs on so she does not have to run around the neighborhood." She pumped her arms like she was jogging.

"Oh, Bella, that's no deep dark secret." I laughed. I was relieved it was something so simple and a little amused that Diana hadn't wanted me to know. She'd wanted to avoid the "be careful" lecture she knew I'd put her through.

"Are you sure you can get these?" Bella asked. "I told her I could have picked up the necklace and dropped these things off. But I think more than anything she needed your company."

"Really, it's no problem at all." I closed the trunk. "And if you need my help, sweetie, you just call me. Between us we'll strap her to a chair if we have to."

"It may come to that," she laughed and waved as I pulled away.

Chapter Nine

WITH THE CONVERTIBLE'S top down I was able to soak in the sunshine and sea air on my way back. I found a classic rock-and-roll station on the car's radio and turned the music up. The Beach Boys' sound was ageless, and "Good Vibrations" seemed like the perfect soundtrack to the drive along PCH. Our beautiful Southern California weather always puts me in a good mood, and this time of day there was very little traffic as I turned my car south and enjoyed the glimpses of the blue Pacific and breaking waves.

I'd called the phone number Bella had given me before I'd left Ruby Point and spoken with Mary Jo, the Laguna Beach Library lady. She said she'd be home if I wanted to come right then. It was on my way to the office so it worked out well for me to swing by en route.

All the cataloguing and organizing of the items for the exhibit had become quite a time-consuming undertaking, she'd said, that had spilled over into evenings during her time off. I knew exactly how those types of volunteer commitments went, having been caught up in a few myself.

The library was small, but they had gotten creative in surviving tough times. This exhibit and the related event sounded like fun. They would have the memorabilia up for thirty days along with books, biographies, and exposes about the Golden Years of Hollywood. They had several stars, Diana among them, coming in for talks, and then the whole event would culminate in a gala with some of the memorabilia and signed books being auctioned off. It was a brilliant idea, and I could see why Diana had been asked to participate.

I found the address easily and pulled up in front of the small white house, parking in the shade. I popped open my trunk and lifted out the boxes Diana had sent. Bella had clearly marked which ones were destined for the library. A quick knock on the door brought Mary Jo, followed by a jaunty little black Scottish Terrier, whom she introduced as Niki. The dog hurried to greet me.

Scottish Terriers are independent and often stubborn, and Niki was no exception. The dogs can sometimes be hard to train because they were bred to work apart from their owners without direction. They often don't do the best in obedience trials because they don't really appreciate direction; they make up their own minds. It takes a strong owner to match a Scottie's independence, but I sensed Mary Jo was up to it.

"So how did you decide to become a librarian?" I asked Mary Jo as we stacked the boxes from Diana on her large dining room table.

"Libraries and books have always been a part of my life from growing up in the Midwest to college, then as a working librarian, and finally a director. Now, my retirement has brought me here."

"It seems like you enjoy the work."

"I really do love it. It's a great library, but it's like a lot of libraries"— she shook her head—"there's never enough money to meet the needs."

"So, this exhibit is also a fundraiser?" I understood being under funded and trying to fill the gap; I'd worked on several events for the Laguna Beach PUPS group, and believe me we'd come up with some interesting events to bridge our funding gap. The annual Cough Up Some Cash Fur Ball was one of my favorites.

"That's right," Mary Jo answered. "My other passion has been classic Hollywood movies, and amazingly we have had quite a few former leading men and leading ladies who have lived right here in our community."

"We have?" I hadn't known that.

"Oh, yes. From George Beranger, the silent film star, to Tab Hunter down the road in Dana Point. And there's Douglas Fairbanks, Jr., and Edith Head, the costume designer, and of course, your friend, Diana Knight.

"I don't know what all Diana sent, but she mentioned a special dress."

Mary Jo began opening boxes. "Oh my, look at this." She pulled out a silver sparkly dress with a full skirt and layers of crinoline. "She wore this in *Little Sis*."

"It's beautiful." I admired the vintage styling. "And it appears to be in great shape."

"I loved that movie." Mary Jo held up the dress. "Diana played a female spy in the British Secret Intelligence Service, which you've probably more often heard referred to as MI6. The title was sort of a play on words. The character Diana played was able to gain all sorts of very helpful intelligence because no one suspected the glamorous 'Little Sis.'" She laughed. "Sorry, my head is full of trivia like that."

"No problem. I'll have to see if I can find a copy of the movie. It sounds like fun."

"Oh, I think you'll love it. I'll loan you my DVD."

"I think there's a book about the making of the movie in here as well." I opened another box. "It's a first edition, signed by the author and the costume designer, and Diana said she signed it as well."

I pulled the book and a note from Diana from one of the smaller boxes. "It looks like from her note that she intends it to be part of the auction."

"Oh, how wonderful!" Mary Jo was clearly excited by the prospect and so was Niki. The little black dog circled and barked as if trying to see what all the excitement was about.

"Hi, there." I rubbed the top of his head. The terrier was a handsome guy. "Have you had Niki long?"

"It's a long story, but my husband and I got him as the result of a Christmas present gone wrong. He was a gift for a two-year-old." She shook her head. "A two-year-old who didn't like his licking and nibbling."

"Go figure, huh?" I shared Mary Jo's view of the questionable decision to get a two-year-old any puppy.

"My husband, Rod, was really the Niki fan. And when he got sick, Niki helped him get moving and on the road to recovery. They had some great times. Since Rod has been gone, Niki and I have taken care of each other."

"Sounds like a Christmas mistake that turned into a wonderful life for Niki." I smiled at Mary Jo.

She paused for a moment. "And for me," she said. "Let's see what else we've got here."

She moved back to the boxes from Diana. Clearly a no-nonsense lady.

I helped her open everything up. She seemed thrilled with Diana's donations, and I knew Diana would be happy they were a hit.

"I understand you were the unfortunate person who discovered the young man who drowned." She gave me a sidelong glance.

I nodded.

"I'm sorry. That must have been very difficult for you."

"Thank you. Yes, it was terrible."

"The two young men, Jake and Cash, donated several computers to the library for public use." She set the last box aside. "I didn't know either one of them well, but they seemed very nice. I hope the police get this sorted out."

"I do, too," I replied. "I guess I'd better be going."

"Well, thank you so much for dropping the items off. I'll get this all logged, and once the event is over we'll send Ms. Knight a receipt for tax purposes." She walked me to the door.

"No problem, I was happy to do it. Good luck with your exhibit." I stepped outside and was walking to my car when Mary Jo called out.

"Oh, wait. I wanted to loan you that movie, *Little Sis,* that Diana is in." She dashed back inside.

I turned my head just in time to see a late-model black SUV pull away from the curb. That did it. I was sure this time. I'd call Detective Malone and see if he was having me followed.

Mary Jo came hurrying out, movie in hand. "Here you go. I think you'll love the movie and enjoy seeing your friend in it."

"Thank you so much." I was still distracted by the SUV. "I'll get it back to you as soon as I can."

I called Malone, not surprised by getting voice mail this time. I left a message for him to call me back, then turned my car toward home. Not taking my usual route, I glanced periodically in my rearview mirror as I drove. The steady traffic was full of SUVs of all colors, but not a dark-colored one that made the same turns I did. Either being followed was a big honking figment of my imagination or my tail was a real pro.

Chapter Ten

ALL DAY IN THE back of my mind, I'd looked forward to beach time that evening with Sam and the dogs. Once home I took a quick shower and changed out of my Stella McCartney and into something better suited for walking along the waves.

The cats had moved from their daytime spot in the sunshine streaming through the patio doors, to their preferred evening perch on the front windowsill in the living room. I put down fresh food and water, and they came to check it out, Thelma and Louise leading the way and Toria trotting behind.

After giving each of them a few pets, I grabbed Dogbert's leash. He paced from me to the door, sensing something special was in store. We didn't have to wait long for Sam to pick us up. I opened the door, and Dogbert shot out in a mad dash for the car.

Sam had brought Mac, his handsome Border Collie and the dog of my dreams. If I had a bigger place, I'd ask Mac to move in.

Dogs settled in the back, we made the short drive to downtown. After circling a few times we found a parking spot. Sam opened the door for me, and I climbed out. The dogs eagerly followed, their noses in the air. They knew where we were and what was in store.

At Main Beach dogs are allowed on the beach in the morning before nine and after six in the evening. We slipped off our shoes and started south, an easy walk on the cool wet sand. We took our time. Dogbert was happy to trot along beside us, easily keeping pace, his tongue hanging out. Mac was a bit more rambunctious. He loved the sand and sea. He'd run ahead, turn and splash in the water a little, and then run back to us. This time of day the beach was full of walkers and their furry family members.

"What's the latest on Jake Wylie's murder?" Sam asked as we ambled along the water's edge.

I filled him in on the events of yesterday. The trip to Jake and Cash's house, the intruder, the return trip with Malone, and the missing equipment.

"I wish we'd hear from Graham Cash again." I paused, watching as the incoming tide brought the waves closer. "There has to be some explanation for his disappearance. If he has been kidnapped, by whom? And why?"

"Do you think the police are still focused on the idea that Cash is to blame?" He picked up a stick and threw it for Mac, and the dog raced down the beach to get it.

Being near the sea is always healing to me. I'm not sure if it's the soothing sound or the vastness, but I felt the stress of the past two days slipping away as the cold water washed over my feet.

"It seems so." I looked out at the deepening colors on the horizon listening to the soft whoosh of the waves. "I don't think they have any other theories."

"Ready to head back?" Sam took my hand.

I nodded and we turned around. An important thing you needed to remember when you parked near the boardwalk and walked the shoreline: you eventually have to walk all the way back to where you've parked your car.

As we approached the Main Beach lifeguard shack and the boardwalk, it got busier. More people, more dogs, more kids. Shouts from a volley game in progress filled the air, and little ones squealed as they climbed on the playground equipment. Sam and I brushed the sand off our feet and sat down on a bench to slip on our shoes. As I dusted the some of the sand from Dogbert's paws, I noticed Wayne, the basset hound fan from the ARL, sitting on the next bench over. He hadn't noticed us but seemed to be people watching.

"Hello, Wayne," I spoke as we passed him. "A nice evening."

"What?" He jumped. "Oh, sorry. Guess I was somewhere else."

"Did I get your name right?" I asked.

"That's right. Why?"

The poor guy was completely lacking in social skills, which I'm guessing might be a barrier to lining up new hedge and tree-trimming clients.

"Wayne and I met a couple of days ago and then ran into each other again today at the ARL," I explained to Sam. "Wayne, this is my friend, Sam." Sam offered his hand, and Wayne shook it. "And this is Mac and Dogbert." I introduced the dogs.

Dogbert was exhausted and took advantage of our pause to rest his paws. Mac was a little standoffish with Wayne, which is unusual for him, but maybe he sensed the big guy only liked basset hounds. Or perhaps it was a bit of a pout on his part because beach time was over.

"Well, the dogs are tired and so am I," I said to Sam. "Shall we go?"

"Enjoy your evening." Sam nodded to Wayne.

We crossed PCH at the light and then walked over to Forest Avenue where the car was parked.

"What does your new friend, Wayne, do for a living?" Sam asked as we walked.

"Chelley at the ARL said he trims hedges and trees," I answered. "His business is called, 'The Cutting Hedge.'"

Sam groaned at the name.

"Why do you ask?" I looped my arm through his.

"Well, I like to think I've got a pretty macho handshake but Wayne's grip may have broken something." Sam smiled as he shook out his fingers. "I'm suddenly feeling like I need to hit the gym." He chuckled.

We'd reached the Ferrari. He opened the passenger door, and the dogs scrambled in the back just as my phone rang. I glanced at the number.

"Detective Malone," I explained to Sam as I pushed the button to take the call.

"This is Caro." Hopefully he was calling regarding the message I'd left him about the police tailing me. If the police were keeping an eye on my comings and goings, I guess I didn't have a problem with that kind of surveillance. I simply thought they should have told me.

"About this vehicle." Malone got right to the point. "Can you describe it?"

"Don't you know what kind of vehicle you sent to spy on me?"

"We don't have anyone assigned to tail you."

I felt the scamper of fear slide down my spine. "It was a dark-colored SUV, a big one, maybe blue, maybe black." I swallowed. "If not your people, then who is following me?"

"I don't know." His tone was serious. "I want you to call it in immediately if you notice the SUV again."

"No problem." I would be happy to make that phone call. "I gather you also spoke with Heidi Sussman, Cash's girlfriend."

"Yes. She was helpful regarding the dispute with the neighbor about the cat."

"Good." I hesitated and there was silence for a few seconds.

"If you have something important to the case, Ms. Lamont, I'd suggest you not keep it to yourself."

We were apparently back to Ms. Lamont.

"It's not something I'm sure is relevant or important. But I overheard a conversation that suggested Jake and Cash had an argument last weekend while out with friends." I paced back and forth on the sidewalk.

"What friends?"

"Well, that's just it. I don't know what friends. The conversation I overheard was between Heidi, Cash's girlfriend, and another girl, who she called Morgan. I suggested to Heidi that she should call you, but if she didn't say anything when you talked to her earlier, she must not think it's important."

"I will check it out."

"Okay. Just thought you should know."

"Thanks." I could tell he was done talking to me.

And that was that. I'd done what I could.

Sam had clearly only heard one side of the conversation, but it was enough to create a worried crease between his handsome brows.

"No need for concern, sugar." I touched his forehead with my finger. "I am staying as far away from this murder case as east is from west."

He smiled and caught my finger. "As far away as you can while keeping the missing guy's cat."

"Truly I am contacting Detective Malone with anything suspicious. That's why I called him about this SUV. It's probably my imagination, but I'm being cautious."

Sam pulled me into an embrace. "You're one smart lady, Caro." He leaned back slightly so he could see my face. "And beautiful and kind. But cautious is never a word I'd use to describe you."

"I'll be careful." I wrapped my arms around him and kissed his temple. "I promise."

"Please do." He touched my cheek with his knuckle and then turned and opened the car door for me.

Chapter Eleven

I UNDERSTOOD SAM'S worry, and make no mistake, I truly was staying as far from the murder investigation as possible. In fact, I was at the point I wished I could scrub my mind of the whole thing. At least for a while.

Since I couldn't, I decided an escape was just what the doctor ordered. However, with commitments scheduled for the rest of the week, there was no chance of hopping a plane for some exotic locale. So, I opted for a movie getaway.

The DVD Mary Jo had loaned me would be perfect. A simpler time, a female spy, and it was one of the few Diana Knight movies I hadn't seen.

I threw on my pajamas, popped some popcorn, and settled into my favorite chair. I'd figured after the kind of day I'd had and the long walk, there was a good possibility I'd fall asleep halfway through, but that wasn't the case.

The film's storyline was intense and not only kept my interest, but had me on pins and needles to the point I found myself gripping the arms of my easy chair.

Diana was a superb and glamorous Annabella Caron aka *Little Sis*, who, after her husband was killed by the Gestapo, vowed to avenge his death by doing all she could for the war effort. She became a part of SIS, the Secret Intelligence Service, which worked in conjunction with other British WWII organizations specializing in espionage and sabotage.

Annabella attended the theater and hosted dinner parties, but on the side gathered information on troop movements and helped to smuggle downed Allied airmen out of occupied France via a network of other women.

After being betrayed by a woman she believed to be an ally, she was captured. But the never-say-die Annabella convinced her guards she was not the woman they were looking for by ditching her spangly silver dress for a cleaning woman's clothes. Mary Jo had been right; the iconic silver dress had played a big part in the movie.

As the credits rolled, I thanked my lucky stars I was friends with such a talented and special lady. This role was probably more Diana than any of her romantic comedies. The big heart, the toughness of spirit, the belief in doing the right thing. All part of the reason I loved her so much.

A bit of forties jazz played in the background as the last of the credits finished.

This movie is dedicated to those who, at great risk to themselves, worked behind the scenes to bring about victory as a part of organizations like SIS, commonly referred to as MI6.

Wow, so I guess, like Mary Jo had said, the Secret Intelligence Service used in the film wasn't fictional. There really had been a SIS and still was, however most of us now knew it as MI6. It made me wonder how much of the storyline was fiction and how much was truth.

"Do you suppose they still recruit beautiful women like Annabella to attend cocktail parties and listen for secrets?" I asked Toria. The snoozing cat on my lap didn't answer.

"Probably not," I told Dogbert who had at least raised his head. "I'll bet it's all done with electronic surveillance, wiretapping, and cyber-spying. They probably recruit geeks like Cash and Jake and their friends. In fact, I'll bet the spies not only don't go to dinner parties, they probably don't even have to leave their homes."

Wait a minute! I jumped up, dumping my popcorn on the floor.

Dogbert and Toria scattered, and Thelma and Louise, across the room on the cat perch, even lifted their heads and opened sleepy eyes to see what had created the excitement.

"SIS," I told Dog. "S—I—S. That was the return address on the package that arrived the day Jake was killed and Cash disappeared. It could stand for the British Secret Intelligence Service."

"Grrr . . . woof!" Dogbert barked at me.

"Well, no. I'm not positive, but I think that's what it said."

Dogbert tipped his head quizzically.

"I can check tomorrow if the envelope is still in their office." I popped the DVD out of the player and put it back in the case. If Jake and Cash had received something from the British Intelligence Service, it could explain a lot. If they were spies, maybe foreign agents had killed Jake and kidnapped Cash.

I know what you're thinking. I didn't miss the stretch it was to think the British Intelligence Service would send a communication via regular package delivery. Still, it was worth checking out, right?

Chapter Twelve

THE OFFICE WAS quiet when I entered, but Verdi was at the desk working. Despite her goth look and burgundy hair, the girl was traditional work ethic personified. Before she'd joined the office we'd gone through a series of temp fails that had us thinking we were never going to find a part-time receptionist that was both efficient and friendly. Verdi was the perfect fit.

"How's your morning going?" I slid the basket of cranberry muffins onto the desk. "I had lunch yesterday with Diana who sent me home with these incredible muffins. I don't dare leave them at my house or I'll eat them all."

"My morning is going better now." She plucked one from the basket and bit in. "What's up with the murthdmph?"

"Let me go put my stuff down, and I'll come back when your mouth isn't full." I smiled at her.

Once I'd dropped my bag and files in my office, I stepped back out front to the reception desk.

"What's the latest?" Verdi had polished off one muffin and was reaching for a second.

"Where to start?" I leaned on the counter. I'd opted for a Emilio Pucci nautical-print cotton dress hoping it would add some cheer to the day, but now I was regretting my choice as the snug fit left no room for more muffins.

I filled her in on going to get Toria's things and my shock when the guy popped out of the wall. I described all the electronic equipment I'd seen in the secret room.

"Sounds like computer servers." She'd polished off a full muffin.

"What does that mean?" Verdi was a lot more familiar with technology than I was.

"A server is just a super-powerful network computer that can share resources with other computers, but that wouldn't be any big surprise given the business they were in."

I wasn't sure I completely understood, but it did make sense that the two would have the type of computers Verdi described.

"It's possible that Cash was kidnapped by the person or persons who killed Jake. I wonder what the guys were working on." She tapped her black-polished nails on the desk as she talked. "Maybe something that their competition wanted to get their hands on."

"Or maybe something involving international intrigue." I told her about watching the movie about British Secret Intelligence and my theory that Jake and Cash were cyber-spies.

"Hmmm. I can't imagine any two more unlikely candidates for spies." She brushed some crumbs into the wastebasket. "I do remember seeing envelopes routinely come for them from a UK address, but I don't remember the sender. I didn't think anything of it. Cash is British after all."

If I wasn't able to convince Verdi, I stood no chance with Detective Malone.

"I imagine police have been through Cash and Jake's office?" I asked. Maybe if I could show her the envelope she'd at least consider the possibility of spies among us.

"I don't know. There isn't any crime-scene tape across the door." She glanced in the direction of the 2Gyz office. "If they did, I wasn't here but I can't imagine they didn't check it out."

"We could just do a quick look and see," I offered. Our eyes met.

"Detective Malone will be really upset." Verdi had some past experience with Malone and his investigations

"I'm sure they've already finished their search." I couldn't think they hadn't been through the office. "If it looks like it's sealed off, we'll leave it alone," I assured her.

I was sure I'd recognize the envelope that I had signed for the day Jake was killed.

"Okay." Verdi unlocked her desk and retrieved the master key to the offices.

She inserted the key in the lock, and we eased open the door of the 2Gyz work space. The desk was bare of its usual clutter, and the computer was missing. The monitor with its alien face on the back had disappeared. There was nothing at all in the room other than the desk and chair.

"I hope the cops did this." Verdi looked around the room.

"Me too." I peered into the office without actually going in.

"Maybe you should call Malone and make sure it was the cops." Verdi leaned in beside me.

"Me?" I'd been talking with the homicide detective a little too frequently. I thought Verdi should make the call. Or maybe a call wasn't necessary. After all, we hadn't actually gone inside.

We turned back to the reception area and were startled by a man standing just inside the door.

Jumping Jehosaphat!

Verdi and I both fell back about a foot. We really did need to get one of those bells that dings when someone enters. The office group had looked at one months ago, but it'd seemed unnecessary. None of us who shared the space had that many walk-ins. Usually.

The man who stood in the entry was middle-aged, medium-height, and not scary-looking in any way, but it was still disconcerting to have people simply appear.

"Can I help you with something?" Verdi asked him.

"Yes, you can." He approached the reception desk. "I need to find Jake Wylie and Graham Cash."

"Not here," I answered. Could it be the man didn't know one was missing and the other was dead?

"Do you know where could I find them?" He pulled a paper from his jacket pocket.

"We don't really know," I answered quickly.

"It appears you know them well enough to be snooping in their office." He indicated the open office door.

Guilty. I could feel my cheeks warm. "Why are you looking for them?"

"Got some papers for them." He tapped the envelope against his hand.

"You're serving them with legal papers?" Verdi asked.

"I am."

"You'll have to stop by the police department for the details, but Jake Wylie is dead and Graham Cash is missing," I blurted out.

He stood silent for a minute as if taking in the information. "Can you direct me to the police station?"

Verdi gave him directions though it wasn't far.

He turned to go.

"What are they being sued for?" I asked.

"Guess it's no skin off my nose." He shrugged. "Seems they copied one of their computer things from somebody else. Or at least somebody thinks they did."

The man turned toward the door again. "Thank you for your help," he said over his shoulder as he exited.

"Whoa." I turned to look at Verdi. "That adds a new twist to things."

"It certainly does." Verdi locked up the 2Gyz office.

Psychic Suzanne walked in through the front door just as Verdi walked around to replace the key in her desk drawer.

"Things are not as they seem," she intoned before crossing to her own office, going in and shutting the door.

Verdi and I looked at each other.

Well, no kidding.

I returned to my desk and tried to concentrate on what I needed to do. I had paperwork to finish and files to update, but my mind kept wandering to what the process server had said. If Cash and Jake were being sued because of a disagreement over an app they'd developed, that would involve a lot of money. Millions maybe. Could it perhaps be enough money to be a motive for murder?

I debated about whether to even follow up with Malone on my cyber-spy theory. At midnight it had seemed reasonable, but it had sounded pretty far-fetched when I tried to explain it to Verdi. She was right; the California surfer boy and the absent-minded British cat-lover did seem like unlikely spy potential.

I'd wrapped up my paperwork and started on my to-do list for the next day when I heard voices out front.

"You can't—wait a minute. You can't just barge in there." Verdi's tone was firm.

"Yes, I can," a voice I recognized argued. "I'm a client, and besides we're working together on the murder case."

Betty Foxx appeared at my office door. Verdi hesitated just outside.

"What are you doing here, Betty?" I nodded to Verdi that it was okay.

"I'm here because it's not working." Today Betty was attired in a dark-plum velour pantsuit, a step up from the usual pajamas, but the pants were hiked up to her armpits. Bright-white tennis shoes completed the outfit.

She crossed her arms across her chest and tapped one bright-white toe in impatience.

"What's not working?"

"The stuff you told me to do with Raider."

I sighed. "Tell me what you've been doing."

"What you told me to do." She rolled her eyes.

"You've been walking Raider?" I asked.

"Yes, I did, but now look at me." She pulled up her pant legs to reveal two skinned knees. "And not only that, I ruined my favorite outfit. The limited-edition, hot-pink, Jackie-O-one I got on sale last month on the shopping channel. It was only for a limited time. It's irreplaceable." Her thin fingers dropped the pant leg with emphasis.

If the O was supposed to stand for Jackie Onassis, I was pretty sure the icon of fashion and good taste had never worn hot-pink PJs, at least not out in public, but that was neither here nor there. The biggest issue was that Betty had been injured, and luckily this time it had been minor. Good grief. She could have fallen and broken a hip or something.

Okay, so Betty was right; my advice had not been the right advice for a petite older woman. Even one as feisty as Betty Foxx.

"You're right, Betty. It's not working."

"Whadda you mean?" Betty huffed. "You still on the 'I'm too small and too old for that kind of dog.' I don't want another kind of dog. I want Raider." Betty paced while she talked.

"Hold on. That's not what I meant. I meant Raider is too big and too young for what I recommended." I watched Betty, considering solutions.

"So what now?" She stopped in front of me. "You givin' up?"

"No. We need to take a different approach." I wasn't ready to throw in the towel. "Do you know where the Laguna Beach dog park is?"

"Yep, out on Laguna Canyon Road."

"Where's Raider now?"

"At home. Probably chewing up his newest stuffed toy from the Bow Wow Boutique. Cookie gives me a discount."

"Can you meet me tomorrow morning at the dog park?"

"I hafta be at work by ten."

I was sure Melinda could spare her if Betty needed to come in later, but it didn't really matter. I could meet her at nine, and we'd have plenty of time. I could stop by the ARL and grab Pharaoh, the Lab, and take him for some exercise like I'd promised Don Furry.

There was a commotion in the outer office. Good grief, we really did need one of those announcement bells.

This time it was Heidi Sussman who burst in, followed by Verdi who was attempting to stop her. She pushed past Verdi, who threw her arms up in surrender but waited in the doorway.

"What did you think you were doing telling the police I was

withholding information?" She was clearly furious, her face almost as pink as her skimpy fuchsia crop top.

"I didn't say you were withholding anything. I simply told Detective Malone the truth. I'd suggest you do the same."

Betty looked from Heidi to me and then back again. She stepped between Heidi and me, facing Heidi. "Wait your turn, chicklet. I'm talking to the pet shrink right now."

"Back off." Heidi stepped forward toward Betty.

"You need to back off and stop acting like a brat." Betty dropped her handbag on the floor and took a defensive stance, her arms raised like she was about to karate chop the younger woman.

Uh-oh. I motioned to Verdi, who closed the door so that the noise didn't disturb Suzanne and the rest of my officemates.

"Ladies." I raised my voice.

"That's no lady." Betty pointed at Heidi. "Look at how she's dressed with her ta-tas about to pop out of her clothes."

I didn't think Betty had any room at all to be criticizing anyone's fashion choices, but Heidi's top was maybe a size too small for her, um, size.

Heidi leaned in nose to nose with Betty. "Listen here, you old bat, for your information this top is a very expensive McQueen."

"I don't care if the McQueen of England herself gave it to you. It looks like you're wearin' your skivies." Betty shook her finger in Heidi's face.

"It's *Alexander* McQueen," Heidi bristled.

"*You* listen here, Missy, you may think you're little Miss Richie from Richistan, but that doesn't give you the right to act disrespectful."

"Time out." I waved my arms between the two like I was refereeing a fight, and I guess I kind of was. "You're both upset. Let's calm down and talk about this."

"I'm done talking." Heidi turned on her heel and stormed out.

"Do you think you might have been a little rough on her?" I looked at Betty.

"I don't care." Betty picked up her handbag from the floor. "I've met better behaved toddlers."

"I agree she said some things that were uncalled for, but mostly because she was upset." I didn't really care that Heidi was unhappy with me. I just hoped she really had been upfront with Detective Malone.

"So you ratted her out to Detective Hottie?" Betty asked.

"Not really." A tap on the now open door saved me from answering. "Am I interrupting?" It was Geoff. Great, the perfect monkey to add to this circus.

And besides, what was the deal? Was my office Grand Central Station this morning?

Geoffrey didn't wait for an answer but strolled on in.

Betty looked him up and down, then sidled up to him and squeezed his forearm with her fingers. "Hubba hubba," she said with fluttering lashes and an exaggerated wink at Geoff, before turning back to me.

"What kind of perfume do you wear, Carol?"

"Why?"

"Must be one of them pheromone ones they sell late at night on the shopping channel, cuz the hunks seem to flock to you like flies."

And with that, Betty blew Geoff an air kiss, and she was gone.

Chapter Thirteen

GEOFF CONTINUED right on in without hesitation. I didn't think the hunks were flocking, but if they were, this was one hunk I wished would fly the coop.

"Who was the bag lady?" he asked. "And what was that on her forehead?"

"Betty is one of my clients, those were her eyebrows, and we should all hope for as much spunk as she has when we're her age."

Yes, Betty was a little bizarre. Big deal. I didn't appreciate his derogatory comments. As crazy-making as she was, I'd take Betty Foxx's company over his any day.

"No house calls today?" Geoff dropped into one of the plum-colored leather chairs next to my desk as if he planned to stay for a while.

I didn't respond to his question, and I didn't sit down. I didn't want Geoff to get the impression he was welcome to stay.

What had I ever seen in the man? Granted he'd been easy on the eyes, and still was. Tall and lean, he wore his custom-tailored, silver-grey suit well. Neatly styled, nearly black hair, chiseled jaw, intelligent dark blue eyes.

But it had never been about his looks. We'd met in college, and he had treated me in a way no other guy had before. Geoff didn't make a big deal of my looks. He'd always wanted to play down the fact that I'd done the beauty-pageant circuit. That was okay with me; I'd hated it. I was young and earnest and in love with the idea of love. I'd been so enamored; I'd been blind to his faults.

I wanted to boot-kick myself.

"No canines or kitties in need of counseling?" He looked around the office. It wasn't large, but I thought I'd done an alright job with the furnishings. In fact, except for the basket of pet toys and the paw-print rug, it could be any therapist's office.

"The pet counseling business must be a lucrative one." He raised a dark brow in what I'm sure he assumed to be a debonair expression.

"I do okay. Now, I've got work to do." I wished he would give it up.

Surely he must realize with what he'd put me through; there were no second chances. Who was I kidding? Of course he didn't realize. His ego was as big as Texas, and he never considered defeat.

"Any news on the murder investigation you're involved in?"

"No, and I'm not involved." I stared at him, wishing my thoughts of his leaving would make him go away.

"Hmmm." Again the thoughtful hand on the chin.

I imagined him practicing it in front of the mirror.

"Geoffrey, what are you doing here?" Sending go-away thoughts wasn't working; maybe the straight-forward approach would move him along.

"My, my. Prickly aren't we?"

"Not prickly, but I've got no time for your hooey."

"Hooey?" He laughed. "Hooey. I'm not even sure what that means. You always had such colorful Texas language, Carolina."

If he didn't leave my office soon, I'd be fixin' to show him some Texas language a whole lot more colorful than "hooey."

"When are you done for the day?" He glanced toward the door. "I don't see any patients waiting. Perhaps we could go to dinner."

"Dinner?" I could feel my face get hot as my temper flared, but I made my voice very quiet. I would not let him get to me. "Geoffrey, I do not want to go to dinner. I do not want you in my office, and if you *ever* show up at one of my in-home appointments again, I will call my friend, Detective Malone, and have you escorted from the premises." I took a deep breath. "Do you understand?"

"My dear, I can see I've caught you at a bad time." He managed to make it sound like he was trying hard to be nice and I was having a hissy fit for no good reason.

He stood and leaned toward me like he might want to kiss me good-bye. My hand itched to slap the smirk off his face, but I resisted.

Geoffrey took my partially-raised hand and lifted it to his lips. "We'll try for another time when you aren't so stressed."

I picked up the stuffed cat toy that lay on my desk and chucked it at his head as he left. The bright-blue mouse landed with a very unsatisfying *thunk* halfway to the door.

Chapter Fourteen

VERDI LEFT FOR the day with a comment about perhaps investing in a traffic-cop uniform for the next time she worked. I thought a referee shirt and a whistle might do the trick.

I began packing myself up to leave as well. My plan was to stop by my house, grab some lunch, take Dog for a short walk, and then I had errands to run. I also needed to call Olivia Fletcher. She was the lady with the Schnauzer that I'd had to reschedule the day there'd been all the excitement with the secret room.

I shut down my computer and gathered my papers.

"Hello." A voice I knew well boomed in the empty outer room. "Is anyone here?"

Really? On top of the previous parade of visitors?

I thought about not answering, but avoiding the reporter seemed childish on my part.

"In here," I finally answered with a heavy sigh.

"Working?" Callum MacAvoy stepped through my office doorway.

"Yes." I looked behind him for his camera crew, but it appeared to only be him. "Is there something I can do for you, Mr. MacAvoy?"

"Mac, please." He dropped into the chair Geoff had just vacated. "My friends call me Mac."

Uhm, no. Mac was Sam's dog. Whom I liked. Callum MacAvoy, I wasn't sure about.

"Is there something I can do for you?" I wasn't going to call him by his nickname like we were friends, but I also wasn't going to waste time arguing about what to call him.

The sooner I could figure out why he'd stopped by and move him along on his way out of my office, the better. It had to be getting close to his noon spot, so I guessed he wouldn't stick around too long.

"You can tell me what the latest is in the murder investigation." He leaned forward as if I could trust him. Like it would be our little secret. Yeah, right. I knew his type all too well.

"You'll have to check with the police." I continued shuffling papers. "I'm sure Detective Malone would be happy to give you an official statement."

"But you're the one with the missing boy billionaire's cat. Have you heard from him?" He tapped his temple. "I'm thinking you have."

"What makes you think that?" I avoided his question, and I could see from his face he knew that's what I was doing. He might be irritating, but he was as smart as a whip.

And as stubborn as a mule. He sat and stared at me.

"You know, MacAvoy"—I met his gaze—"I do have Graham Cash's cat, but I don't know where he is. I just hope he's okay. I have no information to give you."

"I don't think that's true. I think you're knee-deep in this intrigue and you know more than you're saying. I did some checking, and you have an interesting past."

"Really?"

"Former beauty queen. Walked away from all that. Society wedding, marriage to a high-priced Dallas therapist. Then there's a scandal, and it all comes crashing down. Moves to Laguna Beach, starts a new business. Lands Orange County's most eligible bachelor." He rattled off my life in his broadcaster voice.

"Sounds like a made-for-TV drama when you summarize it like that." I kept my voice steady. I recognized his blatant attempt to get a rise for what it was.

"It does, doesn't it?" He dropped back to his normal voice.

"So what's your point?" I looked him straight in the eyes.

"Just that I've got questions."

"I'm sure you do."

"This isn't the first murder investigation you've been involved in, is it?"

"I'm hardly involved, Mr. MacAvoy. Like I keep telling everyone, I'm only the catsitter."

"Still it's odd, isn't it?" His green eyes pinned me.

I shrugged and waited for him to make his point.

"I wonder about things like that. Coincidences."

Again, I waited, but cut eye contact and went back to packing things up for my next appointment.

"Then there's not just you, but the beautiful Melinda and the hint of a scandal in her past."

"Also, none of your business." I dropped my voice to a deadly calm, which would have warned him of the coming explosion if he'd known me better.

"I did some research on your cousin, too. Will she finally be rid of the shady art dealer and find someone better?" He'd slipped back into the voiceover. "And will the scandal from her past—"

"Get out." I stood and pointed at the door.

MacAvoy froze, the expression in his green eyes told me he hadn't seen that coming. He'd thought he was poking a stick at a well-trained pure bred and found out there was junkyard dog in my lineage.

The idiot had crossed a line.

"You can pick on me and drag out all the skeletons in my closet and make them dance if you like, but not my family. You mind your own business, Callum MacAvoy. Melinda is off limits."

MacAvoy blinked and took his time standing. "If you hear any-thing . . ."

"Out."

"Okay, okay. I'm going." He raised his hands in surrender.

Wow. What a slime ball. I probably wouldn't have lost my temper so easily had I not just been through the drama of Betty and Heidi's disagreement, and then Geoff showing up in my office and acting like he could walk back into my life. I was done. I had no use for the press in general and Callum MacAvoy in particular.

Chapter Fifteen

OLIVIA FLETCHER had been willing to reschedule for that afternoon, and I was glad. A dose of my usual routine was exactly what I needed to get my head on straight.

I stopped by home, fixed a salad, and did a quick once-around-the-block with Dogbert. The felines were sprawled, sunning themselves on the windowsill, and I was happy to see Thelma and Louise had made room for Toria.

My stop to work with Olivia and Baymont, her Schnauzer, would be a quick one. When the little of slip of a woman answered the door, I immediately apologized for having to reschedule.

Olivia, a recent widow, led the way to a wicker-filled sunroom. Sunlight and soft colors washed through the dappled room. It seemed perfect for such a gracious and soft-spoken lady.

She'd been working with Baymont on some of my recommendations. He was quite a handsome fellow and had the Schnauzer's unique arched eyebrows and bristly mustache and beard. When he saw me, he barked a deep bark and then went to stand by Olivia as if letting me know he was her bodyguard.

I easily fell into my routine and spent some time with the two, asking questions and observing how they interacted. I reassured Olivia what she was doing was working. Baymont barked a lot, but not excessively. A bit over-protective at the dog park, Olivia needed to curb her own nervousness so Baymont would know the situation was stable and didn't require his intervention. He was Olivia's first dog, and I think she mostly needed tips on how to handle his personality. They would do fine.

The time spent working with Olivia and Baymont had been soothing. This was what I did and who I was. This was the life I'd created for myself here, and I hoped soon Jake's murder and Cash's disappearance would be sorted out and life would get back to normal. I also hoped my ex-husband would tire of his pursuit and take himself back to Texas.

As I left the house, I hesitated a few minutes before getting in my car. Studying the surrounding area, I looked for the dark SUV, but didn't see it. The neighborhood was full of houses with attached garages, and very few cars were parked on the street. I waited a few minutes. Nothing.

Now that I knew it wasn't the Laguna Beach police who were following me, my nerves were even more on edge. Given all that had gone on, I knew in my state of mind, I very well could have imagined it. It isn't like there aren't dark-colored SUVs all over Orange County. Still better safe than sorry, right?

If I spotted the SUV, I would call immediately just like Malone had told me to do. Even if it turned out to be some soccer mom with a black SUV full of kids. So, I'd feel foolish. Wouldn't be the first time.

After leaving Olivia Fletcher's, I couldn't resist. Her place wasn't far from Cash and Jake's neighborhood so I took a little detour and drove by the house. Still no dark vehicle, and I was plenty relieved by its absence.

Of course, I had to admit that after watching *Little Sis*, in my mind I'd concocted a whole international-intrigue scenario where a dangerous undercover spy had killed Jake and then had taken Cash. They were probably holding him hostage and making him work on their secret project. In my imaginings I was vague about the details of the secret project itself. Probably because I knew so few details about the world of computers.

I wondered if maybe the grumpy neighbor's video cameras were angled in such a way he might have caught the spies dragging Cash from the house. Maybe there was something on video that would give my spy theory credence.

As I came to their block, I slowed. I noticed a "Cutting Hedge" van alongside the curb a few houses down and chuckled again at the name. I hoped Wayne was finding work. There were a lot of hardy good-sized bougainvillea hedges surrounding some of the properties, but I imagined many of the homeowners had regular services that handled those types of things. It had to be difficult for someone like him starting up a new business. And, bless his heart, Wayne wasn't exactly Mr. Personality.

I paused in front of the grumpy neighbor's fortress and looked to see if I could spot the cameras. I guessed they would probably be pretty small. Technology keeps getting smaller and smaller. Binoculars would have helped a great deal, but I hadn't planned to drive by the area.

I glanced around at the other houses. Mr. "Cutting Hedge" down the street was unloading some tools, so it looked like he had found some work after all. Good for him.

As I turned back to Cash and Jake's neighbor's house, a shiny black SUV with dark tinted windows pulled into the drive. The garage door silently slid open, and the big vehicle drove inside.

Wait a minute. What if it was the neighbor?

What if it wasn't only the cat the guy next door had objected to? What if he had fought with Jake like the reporter had said, killed him, and pushed him in the pool? What if he was the one who had been following me?

Suddenly, the tall, thin man burst out of his front door and charged toward my car, his face a dark red. I stepped on the gas and sped away, but in my rearview mirror I could see him yelling and shaking his fist.

My heart raced as I hit Malone's number on my cell. It says a lot about the life I lead that I have a homicide detective's number saved in my favorites, but at times like this I was glad I did.

Malone picked up right away, and I pulled over to talk to him. He told me they'd send someone to the house immediately. Needless to say, I didn't share my secret spy theory which, in comparison to the clear and present danger of an angry man chasing me, seemed like sheer fiction.

I was done. I went directly home.

All evening I was on edge waiting for Malone to call. How could he leave me hanging like this? I had tons of questions. What had happened when they went to the house? What had the neighbor guy said? Had they arrested him for Jake's murder?

Dogbert and I did a long walk around the neighborhood, but I made sure I had my cell phone, both for safety and because I was sure Malone would call any minute.

One of the things I love about being so close to the ocean is that even when you can't see it you know it's there. The evening walk calmed me a little. Dogbert stopped and sniffed and marked. We had a sort of companionable rhythm, he and I.

As we walked, I reviewed what had happened the past few days. Since the day I'd discovered Jake in the pool, it was like everything was in hyper drive.

Back home, I rewrote my list for the next day adding all the errands I'd bailed on after my close encounter of the bizarre kind. Then I took a few minutes to take care of one of the other items on today's list I hadn't gotten to earlier.

I settled in on the couch with a glass of sweet tea and dialed Diana's number. I'd been wondering all day how she was doing.

She said she'd had a follow-up appointment that afternoon, and her doctor felt like by the weekend she could go back to her normal activities.

"That's great news, but did you tell him what your 'normal' activities are?" I teased.

"You're one to talk." She laughed. "Say, I ran into your cousin when I was downtown for my doctor's appointment."

"You did?" I kept my voice neutral. "How is Mel?"

Diana hesitated. "Worried about you with your ex in town."

"I can deal with Geoff." Though, in a perfect world, he'd give up and go back to Texas, I mused.

I noticed my neglected houseplants and fetched a watering can from the kitchen. The ponytail palm was shedding, and I picked out the loose leaves. It might have had some feline help. The plant had been a gift, but I had checked it out with the greenhouse to make sure it was safe for pets.

"I don't doubt you can, hon." I felt her grin of confidence come as if she were in the room. She waited for a beat. "One more thing, Caro."

"What?" I stopped mid-stride toward the tall bamboo in the corner.

"Melinda wasn't wearing her engagement ring."

What Callum MacAvoy had told me was true then. I'd hoped it wasn't. "They've broken up before." I reminded Diana.

"True." She sighed. "You know I love you like family, right? So keep that thought in mind as I go sticking my nose in where it doesn't belong."

"Go ahead." I suddenly knew where this was going.

"It's not any of my business, but you girls might think about how nice it would be to have each other to lean on in times like these." Diana's gentle suggestion was heartfelt, and I understood she said it out of love. There was just so darn much to sort out. I didn't know where to start, and probably Mel didn't either.

"I know what you're saying, Di." I swallowed hard. "I'm not sure we're ready, but I appreciate your concern."

We eased away from the topic, and I told her about Jake and Cash's neighbor chasing my car. She agreed Malone should have called with an update. I promised to keep her in the loop, and she promised to take it easy with the "normal" activities. I smiled as we hung up and carried the empty watering can to the kitchen.

When my phone rang, I rushed to pick it up.

This time it was Sam, and I filled him in on the events of the day as well. Like Diana, he was concerned about my safety. I told him I'd call him with an update once I heard from Detective Malone.

The next time my phone rang, it was Mama Kat's ring tone. I answered.

"Carolina, have you checked on those dates yet?" As much as we often don't like to think we're mirrors of our mamas, I knew she held a list in her hand.

"Sorry, Mama." I yawned. "I haven't had time, but I'm pretty sure I can make work whatever date you decide on."

"Now, missy, as much as I'm excited to see you, it's not just your schedule I need you to check." Mama sighed. "You'll, of course, be bringing your young man."

I'd be willing to bet Sam had never experienced an authentic Texas barbecue. At least not a Montgomery-style Texas barbecue. I was sure he'd enjoy it, and I was equally sure the Montgomery clan would welcome him. However, I wasn't sure I was going to invite him to attend this one.

I didn't know if Sam was ready for the drama that was my family. Or maybe I wasn't ready, because once Mama Kat met Sam in person, well, there'd be no stopping that when-are-you-setting-a-date freight train.

Mama must have sensed my hesitation. "I'm going to email these dates to you right now." I could hear the clack of her manicured nails on the keyboard. "There. You check tomorrow and let me know."

We rang off, and I checked my now nearly dead cell phone to see if I'd missed any calls.

Nothing.

I plugged it into the charger, but I knew if I hadn't heard from Detective Malone at this point, I wouldn't hear from him until the next day.

Chapter Sixteen

AS YOU CAN IMAGINE, the first thing I did the next morning was call Detective Malone. I'll give you one guess what I got. That's right, voice mail.

On my way to the dog park, I stopped at the ARL to drop off the donations from Diana and pick up the dogs I'd promised to take along. Diana was such an avid supporter of the shelter and its support group, PUPS. She volunteered, she donated supplies, and, as I mentioned before, she fostered animals that needed special attention, like Barbary, the grumpy one-eyed basset hound who'd started out as a "foster" but who'd been with Diana for over a year now.

I was to meet Betty at the dog park at nine to work with Raider and thought I'd offer to take Pharaoh, the black Lab with me.

As I walked up, my arms full of supplies, Don Furry arrived at the same time, bringing in Pharaoh and an adorable Irish Setter.

"Hi, Don." He held the door open so I could come through. "I thought I'd help get Pharaoh out for some exercise, but it looks like you beat me to it."

"Yeah, sorry, Caro." He ran a hand through his white hair. "I forgot you'd offered until I was already at the dog park. I hope you didn't make a special trip."

"No worries at all, Don." I put the box down on a bench. "I had these supplies from Diana to drop off anyway."

"I think my two buddies enjoyed the chance to run, and I liked getting a bit of fresh air myself before the heat of the day." He shucked off his jacket. "How is our Diana doing?"

"She's doing well, and according to her, she has the doctor's permission to return to normal activities this weekend." I took the opportunity to give the two canines a head rub. Beautiful dogs, both of them, and I wished for good forever homes for them. "I told her I wasn't sure her doctor understood what her normal activities were when he gave her the green light."

"Probably not." Don laughed. "Give her my best when you talk to her. Hopefully we'll see her next week. I'll try to steer her toward desk duty."

"Good idea, Don." When I turned to go, I spotted Wayne at the counter in the outer office filling out some papers.

"Is the gentleman talking to Chelley finally getting his basset hound?"

"Yep, the hold period expires in two days for Cheeky, and he'll be available for adoption. So, he's filling out his papers and putting a hold on him."

"Cheeky?"

"Yes," Don chuckled. "Don't look at me. Chelley started calling the hound Cheeky because she said he has these cute droopy cheeks, and it just stuck. Now she's got us all doing it."

"Hello, Wayne?" I went through and spoke to the man. "I've seen your company van out and about. You seem to be getting some trimming work around town."

"Yeah." Clearly he wasn't the chatty type.

"So, you've decided to adopt."

"I have to fill out these forms and wait a while more."

The rescue had a strict policy to ensure that the pets were adopted into a safe and secure environment. They had to be sure the animals weren't adopted by those who would use and abuse them, but they also had to protect against well-intentioned people who truly wanted to adopt but were unprepared to take care of their new family member.

I was glad the slightly overweight basset hound was getting a good home. I had been convinced he would be claimed by his owners.

The basset hound had been at the shelter for eight days, and we only hold pets for ten before we move them to adoption. So, he was soon going to be available.

"So you're adopting Cheeky?"

"Yes, I used to have a basset hound."

I remembered he'd mentioned losing a basset hound. I felt for anyone who had to deal with the loss of a faithful friend. I didn't know what I'd do without Dogbert, Thelma, and Louise. Maybe that's why I was so convinced Cash wouldn't just up and leave his cat.

"Cheeky's a great dog. He won't give you any trouble at all. But he does need a little exercise." I smiled at the guy. "He's lost a couple of pounds since he's been here but could stand to lose some more."

He turned and gave me a hard look. Maybe he thought I was commenting on his size. I hadn't meant to offend him but felt I needed to mention Cheeky's health. The sweet basset hound was a little tubby and a lot lazy and truly needed to get out more.

"I'm sure Mr. Kemper will take Cheeky for walks," Chelley interrupted. "Won't you, dear?"

"Yes." He turned his back to me and returned to his paperwork.

I gave Chelley a sorry-I-interrupted look and moved to leave. I needed to get to the dog park anyway.

It was good when there was a person waiting in the wings for an abandoned pet. It wasn't always so easy, and often an older dog like Cheeky would be passed over for a cute little puppy.

I let myself out, slid behind the wheel, and exited the parking lot onto Laguna Canyon Road toward what many of the locals referred to as "The Bark Park."

I'D ASKED BETTY FOXX to meet me at the dog park because I thought it would be best to demonstrate how Raider could get exercise without Betty exhausting herself. Or getting injured again.

I had no idea how old the spritely lady was, but whatever her age, I was concerned there was a real danger she could break something in a fall caused by such a large dog.

As I drove down the road to the park, my thoughts turned to Jake and Cash's neighbor and the black SUV. I hoped to hear from Malone.

Suddenly a blue Mini Cooper passed me going way too fast.

Hey there, buddy. Way too fast. Probably some kid.

Heidi had acted like she didn't know anything about what Cash and Jake had been working on. But I had the sense that though she liked to play at being an airhead, there was more than just empty air under those expensive blond highlights.

If they'd truly been in a legal battle as the process server had indicated, was it possible the other party had taken drastic measures to win? Or maybe that hadn't been the intent, but there'd been an argument and Jake had been pushed into the pool.

Yeah, right.

There was the small matter of that electric cord wrapped around his neck. Hard to argue for an accident.

So, now we were back to the bad-tempered next-door neighbor. Or my spy theory.

The Laguna Beach Dog Park has no lot for cars, and so the parking is confined to meters along the canyon road in front of the entrance. I found a spot and parked my Benz, then reached in back for my bag. Up ahead I could see a woman pulling on a leash in an obvious attempt to remove a large barking dog from her very small car.

To my surprise it was the blue Mini Cooper that had passed me.

I quickly locked up and hurried forward to assist her.

Once I got close enough, I realized it was Betty. "Come on, Raider. Come on." She tugged on the leash, but the Saint Bernard just barked in response. Betty reached into her pocket and held up a treat, and all of a sudden the dog bounded from the car knocking her to the sidewalk.

Exactly what I'd feared. I moved quickly to Betty who sat on the walkway. She looked unhurt but a little dazed.

"Sit." I took Raider's leash from her hand.

"I am sitting, Carol." The little sprite was decked out in pearls and silk pajamas. She must have a closet full of PJs and not much else. This set was highway-road-sign yellow. Her attire no longer shocked me. The bright-red eyebrows took a little more getting used to.

"Caro," I corrected. "I meant the dog, Bertha." Two could play at this name game. I took the package of dog treats from her hand. "We agreed no treats when Raider is behaving badly."

"Betty," she corrected and eyed me from her spot on the walk. "He's not behaving badly." She and the dog looked at me with equal reproach. His big head tilted as if he was trying to understand what the problem was.

"Yes, he is. He didn't respond to your command, and he knocked you down."

"Respond to my command? He's not a minion; he's my friend." She brushed at the legs of her pajamas and moved to get up. "No wonder you and Cookie don't get along if you think your friends are supposed to 'respond to your commands.' Geez Louise, lady."

I offered my hand to help her, but she ignored it, straightened her pearls, and got to her feet. Awkwardly, but under her own steam.

Wow, this was not going at all as I'd planned. How could I get through to her?

"Betty, here's the deal. We've got to help Raider understand that he needs to listen to you and respond to what you ask him to do."

By this time the dog had circled around and stood behind Betty. His big doggie grin said, "That was fun. What now?"

"He's just strong-minded." Her jaw jutted forward. "I like that about him."

Someone was strong-minded, aka stubborn, but I didn't think it was

Raider. "That may be, but we need to redirect his strong mind into things that will keep him and you safe."

"Yeah."

"The question is do you want my help or not?"

She eyed me. "Okay, let's get going. I got stuff to do."

With Raider barely containing his excitement, we went down the walkway, crossed the short bridge, and stepped into the dog park. The double-gated entrance allowed us to go in without the danger of other dogs escaping. Once in, I directed Betty and Raider to the left where there was an area for large dogs. A whippet and a Weimaraner rushed forward to sniff Raider and then took off across the open space. Immediately Raider ran after them, yanking the leash from Betty's hand.

The good news was he'd acted so quickly that she didn't have time to resist and therefore wasn't injured. The bad news? The big guy was running around the dog park trailing his leash behind him.

"Raider!" I called. He turned his head and looked at me and then went on chasing the other dogs who ran in ever-widening circles.

"Raider!" Betty yelled, her voice shrill and piercing. She took off across the field, her little pajama-clad legs moving like a wind-up toy. Although the dog park was green space, it was still canyon and therefore rough.

Aye-aye-aye. I took off after Betty, afraid she'd do a face plant in the rough terrain. Every time we got close to Raider he galloped away.

Once we caught Raider and unhooked his leash, we were both out of breath. I suggested we park ourselves on one of the benches and let him run.

"If you can bring him here at least once a week, it will really help him use up some of that pent-up energy," I explained. "However, there are some things you want to watch for."

"Like what?" Betty wriggled herself back on the bench and looked at me.

"For instance, it's normal for the dogs to sniff each other. They're just saying hello."

"Yeah, they do that all the time when they come into the store."

"But if it looks like there's a problem, you need to intervene and call Raider to you immediately. That's why it's so important that he respond to your commands."

"What kinda problem? You mean like fighting?"

"Raider's still a pup and not an aggressive dog, so he probably won't start anything, but sometimes in situations like the dog park there are bullies."

"Kinda like in real life, huh?"

"Exactly." I smiled. "And you have to help keep him safe by training him to do a couple of things. One is to come to you when you call him and the other is to 'leave it' which is basically just getting him to let go of something when you tell him to."

"I can do that." Her silver head nodded.

"It's a great time to use those treats he's so fond of." I indicated the package she had stuffed in her purse.

"Gotcha, Carla."

"Good, Beatrice." I met her eyes. "So, let's start with coming when you call him. We need to start with small steps that you can practice when you're at home."

"Okay, like what?"

"Whether it's a young pup like Raider or an older dog, the first thing you want to do is plant the idea that coming to you is the best thing in the world."

Betty tipped her head like a dog.

"It's not difficult, but simple recall training takes repeating it over and over until it's automatic," I went on. "Any time Raider comes to you, whether you've called him or not, let him know you appreciate it. It doesn't have to be treats, you can shower him with praise or rub his head, which he seems to really like."

"I guess that makes sense."

"If you have trouble getting him to do it at first, don't get discouraged. You've got to catch him doing what you want and then reinforce that behavior."

We both looked at Raider romping with the other big dogs. Exercise was still key, but Betty had to do some very basic training with him or he was going to develop bad habits that would be difficult to get rid of.

"One thing you can try if you can't get him to come is to go in the other direction when you call. Dogs can't resist chasing you; it's play to them. This can be important if he's gotten away from you or is running toward the street. If you run after Raider like we both did earlier when he got away, he's going to keep running away. He thinks you're playing. But if you call him and go the other direction, he's more likely to come toward you."

"So, I go away from him to get him to come to me?" Betty sounded skeptical.

"Another thing, if you save a special treat Raider loves for when you're working with him on recall, you'll probably get better results. Cooked chicken pieces or something like that maybe. My pooch, Dogbert, loves cheese so I used bits of cheese when I first started working with him."

"My friend Luis used chicken to get Barney to run faster during the Dachshund Derby." Betty seemed encouraged.

"Dogs are just like us humans." I was keeping an eye on Raider's location as we talked. So far so good. "The things we enjoy are pretty motivational."

"Yeah, but what if it doesn't work."

"I'll bet it will work." I patted her thin hand. "You just have to start small. Get him to come to you from the kitchen to your living room. Then try doing the same thing in your backyard. Then after he's responding at home, try the dog park."

"I never had a dog. I didn't know there was so much to it." She leaned back on the bench. "But he's worth it."

"Of course, he is." I leaned down to pick up my bag. "I have some books at home on dog training that I used when I first got my dog. They were really helpful to me. If you like, you can borrow them."

"Okay, yeah. Books would be good." She suddenly sat up straight. "Hey, isn't that the cutie cop?" Betty pointed.

She was right; it was Detective Malone making his way across the grounds. Black T-shirt, black jeans, his long legs eating up the space as he strode in our direction.

"Ms. Lamont, Ms. Foxx." Malone stopped in front of where we sat. "I stopped by your office and Verdi told me you had planned to come here."

"I waited for you to call last night."

"It took a while to sort things out." He glanced over at Betty whose wide eyes said she'd taken that the wrong way.

"Maybe you'd like to frisk me, Detective." Betty wiggled her red eyebrows and snickered at her own joke.

Malone just ignored her. "I need to speak to you, privately?" He waited for me to step a few feet away.

"What is it?"

"I spoke with the process server. The letter he was delivering was an intent to sue. The two guys, Jake and Cash, are named in reference to a pet-fitness program they created. Are you familiar with WoofWalker?"

"Yes, I am. It's one of many of those types of programs. I know of at least five or six." I shaded my eyes from the sun to look up at him. Malone was one of a handful of people who made me feel petite. "They generally work just like the people versions, keeping track of activity and sometimes other health information." I hadn't been aware that Jake and Cash had created WoofWalker.

"It seems some guy believes they stole his idea."

"I don't know how that could be. Their device isn't that much different from the rest of the activity monitors out there, and there are a ton."

"Apparently the one Cash and Jake developed does more. It also monitors food intake and other health data." Malone shrugged.

"So who is suing?"

"It's a Brody Patton. Does the name mean anything to you?"

"No, it doesn't." I wondered how this Brody Patton would prove they'd stolen his idea.

Betty popped up between us. "Is this about the murder?" She looked up at Malone and batted her eyes. "I can help you out, Handsome. I'm good at this detecting stuff. Remember when we worked together and solved the murder at the Dachshund races? We were hot on the trail of a killer."

"Go." Malone pointed. "I need talk to Caro."

Betty reluctantly stepped back toward the bench, muttering under her breath.

He took my arm and steered me a couple of steps in the other direction.

"We checked out Jake and Cash's next-door neighbor. According to his vehicle registration, Mr. Zellwen has a brand-new black Escalade."

"His name is Zellwen?" Out of the corner of my eye, I could see Betty inching toward us.

"He had already contacted the department to file a complaint." Malone had his back to her, so he didn't see her moving closer and closer to where we stood.

"A complaint? But how is that possible? Toria is at my house. She was nowhere near his yard and couldn't have bit him." I was outraged for the falsely accused kitty.

"Mr. Zellwen's complaint isn't about the cat; it's about you."

"Me?"

"Yes." I could tell he was holding back a smirk, and I didn't appreciate it. "He believes you are harassing him."

"I was on the street in public space. I was not in his yard, but if I were, I might bite," I added.

"When I called him back, I questioned him about his surveillance recordings."

"And?"

"We could get a court order if we have to, but Zellwen agreed to voluntarily turn over the recordings."

"That's good, right?"

"It is. We'll look at the day of the murder as well as the day you were at the house and encountered the intruder."

"Hopefully you'll find something helpful."

"If we find something, we may need you to stop down at the station."

"I can do that."

"That's it then. I wanted you to be aware. And get your take on the dog-tracking device." He turned to leave and ran smack dab into Betty who had moved to stand directly behind him.

"I gotta get going if I'm gonna get Raider back home before Cookie sends out a search party for me." Betty was unapologetic about her eavesdropping.

"Raider?" Malone looked puzzled.

"Yeah, that's my dog." Betty pointed out the Saint Bernard.

"That's your dog." Malone looked at me.

"We're working out some issues," I explained.

I helped Betty round up Raider and got the leash firmly clipped to his collar then handed the lead to Betty. The big dog's bushy tail whipped back and forth, and he gave Betty's wrist a slobbery lick. He'd definitely enjoyed his outing.

"You can walk me to my car." She looped her arm through Malone's. "We can discuss this new murder investigation."

He turned to look at me.

"Are you coming?" he asked.

I ignored his pleading look. "You guys go on ahead. I see someone I need to speak with."

"I'll be getting those books from you, Carla," Betty threw over her shoulder.

"Anytime, Bertha."

Malone looked confused.

"Don't ask," I told him and smiled at Betty.

She smiled back and tugged on his arm. "Come on, Handsome."

I could hear Betty chirping happily about her theories on the murder investigation. Malone's voice was too low for me to hear, but the pointed look he shot over his shoulder at me was unmistakably clear. It said, *Paybacks are hell, Caro.*

I waved and went to look for a varmint I'd noticed earlier when I was helping Betty corral Raider.

Geoffrey Carlisle was sitting on a bench in the little dog area. He was chatting up one of the dog owners who happened to be a client of mine.

I closed the gate behind me on the big-dog side and let myself into the little-dog area. I greeted a couple of people I knew and then walked to where Geoff was yucking it up with Davia Sinclair. Her dog, Nano, a sweet little Chihuahua, had some depression issues a month or so ago, and I'd been working with them for a while. We were able to get Nano off the anti-depressants she'd been on, and at last check-in she'd been doing well.

I was encouraged she had Nano at the dog park. Although, she wasn't really getting any exercise. She sat in the shade at Davia's feet.

I was a strong advocate for making sure pets get plenty of exercise, but I have to tell you in the pampered world of Bark Mitzvahs, pet spas with paw soaks, peticures, puppy pawlish, and even nannies to get dogs and cats to their playdates, it was often a hard sell.

"Hi, Davia." I greeted her, but ignored Geoff.

It's hard to define why I was so offended at his presence. It was a public dog park after all, and he could certainly go anywhere he wanted and talk to anyone he chose.

Wait. I take back what I said before.

It really wasn't all that difficult to define what sent me over the top about Geoff's reappearance in my life. I did know why it bothered me. I'd come to Laguna Beach to get away from my past. To start fresh. And I'd done it on my own terms. I'd created a new life, and the last thing I needed was a visit from the Ghost of Mistakes Past.

Taking a deep breath, I regrouped in my head.

Leaning down to pet Nano's sleek crown, I asked, "How are you, girl?" She raised her head and gave a little woof.

"She seems to be doing well." I addressed Davia.

"Very well," she replied. "Have you met Geoffrey Carlisle? He's new in town, and he was just telling me about his expertise in dog therapy. He has a Master's degree in psychology and has worked with some celebrities. Oh, I forgot," she tittered. "You can't talk about them."

"Patient confidentially," Geoff intoned. He smiled at Davia and reached down to pat the sleeping pooch.

Well slap my head and call me stupid. It suddenly occurred to me what the louse was up to. Why he'd followed me to a client appointment, why he'd shown up at my office, and why he was hanging out at the dog park.

Talk about a ten-gallon ego. Mr. Geoffrey Carlisle wasn't trying to win me back. He had decided my pet-therapy practice, the business he'd been so derisive about, was a good gig, and he wanted in on the action.

The problem was he'd missed one really important point. I didn't do it for the money. I did it because I loved the animals. Geoff loved no one but himself.

I was madder than a mule with a mouth full of bumblebees, and I had to get out of there fast or I was going to come unglued right on the spot.

I ran through several scenarios in my head and came up with nothing that was appropriate to say in front of a client. Even one who had been so easily mesmerized by Geoffrey's snake-charmer ways.

Deep breath. I put on my very best Texas Miss Congeniality pageant-contestant-under-pressure smile and said a tight but civil good-bye to Davia.

I didn't look in Geoffrey's direction at all. I tried to imagine he was a bug. A small insignificant bug.

I turned and walked away, holding on to my composure until I knew I was out of sight.

Then I stomped out of the park to where I'd parked my car.

People. Some of them turn out better than you hope, and others are just a complete and utter waste of space.

I DIDN'T SEE GEOFFREY the rest of the day, but my realization of what he had been up to still nagged me hours later as I finished up my day.

I had returned phone calls and taken care of a couple of errands, but couldn't shake the cloud hanging over my day. The past week had been overwhelming and much of it utterly and completely out of my control.

It was enough to make any sane person plum crazy.

Jake's murder. I knew Malone and company were working every angle and were frustrated with the lack of evidence. Or even a direction.

No real leads. Nothing at the house that helped. No word from Cash. But, as Malone liked to point out, not mine to worry about.

My ex. I'd started over and made a life. Now, it felt like Geoffrey was intent on robbing me of the hard-won peace of mind I'd created. It wasn't so much about the business. There was plenty to go around. It was more about his motives and why he'd chosen to come here. I felt like my safe haven had been invaded, and in a way, it had.

There was Mama. Her increasingly frequent phone calls kept me on edge. She was on a mission with this family-reunion barbecue, and I knew how that usually worked out for me. I needed to decide whether I was going to do battle on this one or write it on my calendar and be done with it. Just a long weekend, right? But how many months after that would it take me to untangle myself from the lasso that I knew would rope me right back into the family drama. The drama I'd tried so hard to escape?

And Sam. Oh, my. There was a tough one. Things were changing between us. Nothing stays the same, and it shouldn't. Most anyone would call it a good and natural change, but was I ready for it? I could fight it, ignore it, or begin to let it change me.

I pulled into my driveway, glad to be home, but not looking forward to an evening of chasing my worries around in my head.

Sometimes a run on the beach helps me clear my thoughts. So after taking care of pet needs, I changed into shorts, a T-shirt, and my running shoes. I grabbed my water bottle and started for the door.

Dogbert raised his head expectantly.

"Not this time, buddy." I patted his head. "The pace I'm planning on wouldn't work for you."

I parked my car close to where Sam and I had parked the night before and started south down the beach at a good steady speed. I tried to push everything—Jake's murder, my ex, Mama Kat, and where Sam and I were going—from my mind. I tried not to think of anything but the pounding of the surf and the breeze in my hair.

Having gone what I judged to be about a half-mile, I turned and began my run back toward Main Beach and the boardwalk. I don't know that I'd truly cleared my head, but it had made me feel better to take a break from trying to figure things out.

I couldn't do a thing to help with the investigation but pass on the information people shared with me. There wasn't much I could do about Geoffrey. It was a free country, and he could start a business wherever he chose. My mother issues went way back to my pageant days, but we'd come to a détente of sorts. She didn't always get the boundaries, but I could remind her. And Sam. Well, it was going to take more than a run on the beach to sort out that one.

As I approached Main Beach, I slowed. A good, tiring run. Maybe I'd sit down for a minute or two and catch my breath before I walked to where I'd parked my car.

I spotted Wayne, or Mr. Cutting Hedge as I thought of him, sitting on the same bench where he'd been the evening before.

"Hello, Wayne." I approached. "May I share your bench for a couple of minutes?"

He begrudgingly scooted over. I took a drink from my water bottle and let my breathing slow.

"A nice night," I noted, once I was breathing normally.

He jumped and turned to look at me as if he had just remembered I was there.

"Sorry, I didn't mean to interrupt your thoughts."

"I'm not very good with people."

Poor guy. I bet he'd been told that a time or two.

"Do you have family, Wayne?" I'm not sure what compelled me to ask, maybe because I'd never seen him with anyone. He was always alone.

"No," he answered slowly. "I lost my wife."

"I'm sorry." I didn't touch him, remembering his reaction when I had at the shelter.

"I'm getting the basset hound." His voice was flat, like maybe he was afraid to get too excited about the prospect.

"That's great." I hoped he was right. "Dogs are great companions."

We sat in silence for a while, but not a comfortable one. Obviously the big guy had had some sad times in his life. Sad times he perhaps hadn't worked through yet. I wanted to recommend some grief counseling, but there was a line I didn't feel it was right to cross. He hadn't asked for my help, hadn't even really given me an opening.

Finally, I stood. "Good luck with adopting your basset hound, Wayne." I waited for him to look up, but he didn't. "If there's anything I can do to help I will."

He lifted his head, and I remembered the day he'd wandered into the office needing to use the phone because of his car trouble. Who would have thought our paths would cross again?

I stopped at Whole Foods on my way home and grabbed the ingredients for a new cat-treat recipe I wanted to try. I'd had good success with my homemade dog treats, but so far not only did my clients' felines not clamor for my cat treats, Thelma and Louise were also unimpressed. Maybe Toria would be a more helpful treat tester. And maybe a little time baking would take my mind off wondering where Toria's owner was and when he might be coming back.

Chapter Seventeen

THE NEXT MORNING I woke up with two dozen each of Catnip Cookies and Southern Kitten Chick N Biscuits waiting to be cat-tested. And a renewed sense of personal resolve.

No wonder I'd been so low, the past few days had been what Grandma Tillie would have called crazy-making days. The unwelcome interest in my personal life from the TV reporter, the black SUV following me, the complaint about me from Cash and Jake's wacko neighbor, and then Betty, the dog park, and my realization about my ex. The crazy train had been full-throttle, and there'd been plenty of passengers on board.

I was upset with myself for not seeing through Geoffrey and what he was doing. And I was beyond irritated with Mr. TV for his tabloid techniques.

My reaction to the reporter and his digging into Mel's past was telling, wasn't it? Maybe Diana was right and it was time to sit down and have a heart to heart with Mel and sort out this brooch thing. I had the feeling that until we came to grips with all the baggage that piece of family jewelry represented, Mel would keep breaking up with Grey and I'd continue to keep Sam at arm's length.

I didn't even turn on the television as I got ready for the day. I was afraid if I had to listen to Callum MacAvoy on the news, I might end up causing harm to my TV.

I went through my usual morning routine. I took faithful Dogbert for his morning walk, acted as on-call servant to the household's feline needs, and then showered and dressed. I pulled out a bright-turquoise long-sleeved organic cotton tee and my black skinny jeans.

Mary Jo had left me a message and invited me to stop by and see the Golden Days of Hollywood exhibit in its early stages. She had catalogued everything and now was in the process of setting up at the library. She thought I might enjoy a preview.

I put that at the top of my list for the day because it was on my way, and it would also give me the opportunity to return her movie.

The Laguna Beach Public Library was on Glenneyre, near my office, and I was a frequent visitor so I knew my way around. Mary Jo stood just inside the entrance at the Information Desk. I handed her the *Little Sis* DVD. I told her how much I enjoyed it and that I got a kick out of seeing the dress Diana had donated in the film. One of the nearby clothing shops had loaned the library a mannequin, and the dress was displayed along with the book Diana had signed. I loved the frock even more now that I'd seen the movie and knew its history.

I didn't tell Mary Jo that the movie had sent me off on the wild hair of thinking Cash and Jake were spies. At midnight, with the movie and its intrigue fresh in my head, the idea had seemed brilliant. After listening to Verdi point out all the holes in my theory, it was losing its shine.

I took a few minutes to walk through and admire the display cases that were taking shape. What a creative idea to spark interest in some of the books in their collection and also raise some funds for the library.

My office was just a hop, skip, and a jump away, so I swung by there next. Verdi wasn't in today, and I missed her presence. The place seemed eerily quiet after the parade of people the previous day.

I let myself into the building, unlocked my office, and got down to work.

There was a quick rap, and Sam popped his head in my door.

"You're up and about bright and early today," I greeted him. He was looking dress-for-success handsome in a dark-blue Giorgio Armani suit and crisp white shirt that contrasted very nicely with his dark coloring.

"I'm on my way to a business meeting with some of Yia-Yia's cronies. I thought I'd stop by and bring you a coffee on the off chance you hadn't had enough caffeine." He kissed my cheek and handed me a to-go cup from the Koffee Klatch.

I ask you, what's not to love about this guy?

"Oh, sugar, thank you." I took a big sip and sighed. "Perfect. You know my weakness. Now, you'll never get rid of me; I'll follow you anywhere."

"I'm counting on that." He smiled and leaned in for a proper kiss. "How goes the investigation? Have you heard anything?"

"I'm still waiting to hear from Malone on the neighbor, Zellwen's surveillance recordings. I don't know if they have anything for me to look at."

"Wait a minute." Sam dropped into the chair beside my desk. "The neighbor's name is Zellwen?"

"That's right." I inhaled the hot coffee aroma and took another sip. "Is his first name Erich?"

"We could check with Malone." I didn't remember him mentioning a first name. "Why? Do you know him?"

"If it's Erich Zellwen, not only do I know him, I fired him." Sam leaned forward. "Or rather I fired his security company. They were the firm handling security for our Long Beach warehouse. Not a very personable guy to begin with, and then he was just plain insulting to one of our employees. The warehouse manager asked him to apologize, and he flipped out on him."

"Well, that would explain how he's able to afford a house in Jake and Cash's neighborhood. I had wondered about that." I set the to-go cup down on my desk. "And it would also explain all the video surveillance capability. It seemed like overkill to attempt to catch a trespassing kitty cat."

I dialed Malone and asked about the neighbor's first name. He confirmed it was Erich, and I explained Sam's knowledge of the security company Zellwen owned, then handed my phone to Sam so he could fill in the rest of the story.

Sam repeated what he'd told me.

They finished talking, and Sam returned my phone with a smile and a slight lingering of his fingers on my hand.

Malone was still on the line. "We picked up the video surveillance recordings this morning and will begin reviewing them. Could you stop by sometime today?"

"I can be there in about fifteen to twenty minutes. Will that work?"

"It will," he confirmed, and we hung up.

I put my phone down, and it immediately rang. I looked at the number and realized that, in all the excitement, I'd completely forgotten that I owed Rebecca Tyler and her company an answer. I'd had a phone-call discussion with her a couple of days before Cash disappeared and I found Jake in the pool. Since then life had gone a little crazy, and I'd apparently put her offer completely out of my mind.

"Sorry," I mouthed to Sam. "I need to take this."

He smiled and shrugged.

"Hi, Rebecca. I'm so sorry I haven't gotten back to you."

"No problem, but we'd like to know soon if you're in or out."

"I'll definitely let you know in the next few days," I told her. Either I was interested or I wasn't. I needed to make up my mind and not leave her hanging.

She thanked me and said good-bye. I ended the call.

"A new client?" Sam asked.

"No. An unusual opportunity to audition for a reality show called *Pet Intervention*."

"In LA?"

"The audition is in Seattle. I'm not sure if they'll do all the taping there or somewhere else. It would be an opportunity to work with problem pets in a new way." I picked up a pen and added a call back to Rebecca Tyler to my to-do list. "The way I understand it, I'd meet the dog and owner and then work to correct the problem. But I don't know if it's something I want to take on."

"I think it sounds like the perfect fit for you. You'd get to do something you do well, and reach even more people."

"I'm really not sure what I think. It's not even a given that I'd be chosen." I tapped the phone I still held. "I need to let her know in the next few days if I'm interested in auditioning."

"Your choice, of course, but I think you'd be phenomenal."

"Thanks, Sam." I appreciated his confidence in me. He was right; it would be an opportunity to reach a lot more people, but with all that had gone on in the past week, I hadn't had the presence of mind to decide how I felt about the idea. "What did Malone think about your information on the neighbor?"

"Well, just having a bad temper doesn't mean he killed Jake Wylie, but it sure means there's more follow-up that's needed. Malone is going to check out where Zellwen was the day Jake was killed."

"I'll be interested in what he finds out."

"I will also." Sam rose and touched my shoulder. "I've got to get going. You never know what the traffic will be like. Let me know how things go with viewing the videos."

"I will." I smiled at him. "Good luck with your meeting."

"Thanks." He perched on the edge of my desk and waited for me to stop fidgeting. "And, Caro." He took my face gently in his strong hands. His thumb stroked the worried crease in my forehead. "Don't worry. When you're ready, you'll know." He leaned in and kissed me, and then he was gone.

And I was left wondering whether he meant the reality show or us.

Chapter Eighteen

THE POLICE STATION was less than five minutes from my office. I parked out front and entered the low brick building. It housed City Hall, the police department, and the fire department. A neat and tidy lineup of official Laguna Beach services.

Inside, Sally and Lorraine were at the front desk. Why, yes, I am on a first-name basis with staff at the Laguna Beach Police Department. In addition, I am ashamed to admit that we hadn't exactly gotten off on the right foot initially. But I now considered them friends.

"Hey Lorraine, it's our favorite pet shrink," Sally called over her shoulder to the taller woman who stood sorting papers at the back desk.

"How's Buster?" I asked Lorraine.

"You know pugs." She grinned. "He's such a clown. Look at this." She came forward to show me a picture on her phone of Buster in a new vest she'd made him.

"Treats him like a child," Sally teased.

"Well, Buster is like a child to me." Lorraine was unfazed.

"You here to see Malone?" Sally asked.

"I am," I confirmed. "I think he's expecting me."

"He is, hon. You can go on back." Lorraine pointed at the hallway that led to the staff offices. "You know where he is."

"Do you need a coffee or anything?" Sally asked.

"No thanks, sugar. I'm fine." I moved down the corridor to where Malone's office was located. It was small and practical: a desk, a chair, and a file cabinet. He looked up as I entered.

"Good." He stood. "Come with me."

He led me to a room set up with computers and monitors. Much less equipment than had been in the secret room at Jake and Cash's house, but still impressive.

I noticed Cash and Jake's distinctive office computer on a table at the back, the alien's face on the monitor branding the machine as theirs. I'd been sure the police had removed the computer from their office, but I was glad to have confirmation it had been Malone and company.

And not the intruder or the angry neighbor. Or the secret spies.

A young female technician was at the console. She wasn't in uniform, and I didn't know if she was a police officer or not, but she seemed to know her way around a computer.

"Joanne, would you queue up the video for Ms. Lamont?"

"You bet." She made a couple of clicks, and the video began. "This is the day of the murder."

The recording showed the back side of the fence that surrounded the rear of the house. She let it run for a while and then moved the cursor and zipped through several hours. There was no action for a while, and then a shadow was visible. A person.

"Slow it down here." Malone shifted to allow me to scoot forward. "This is about an hour before you arrived at the house."

It was fuzzy, but there was definitely someone lurking in the alleyway.

"It's hard to see, but is that another person?" I pointed at another shadowy figure.

"Let me enlarge it." Joanne stopped the video and made the still shot bigger.

Instead of helping, it made the outline of both figures even less clear.

"Take a close look," Malone encouraged.

"The first person is about the right size to be the guy who was in the house the day I went to get Toria's things." I tried to focus my eyes and see if I could pick out anything distinctive. "But I don't see anything that would allow me to say I think it's definitely him. He never looks up, so you can't see his face."

I was disappointed. It seemed unbelievable to me that someone had entered the house, murdered Jake, and yet even with a recording there was no clear view of the person or persons. That wasn't how it worked on the television crime shows. The killer always looked up at the camera.

"Can you move forward to when the medics arrived?" Malone asked.

"Sure, that's about here." The woman made a couple of more clicks, and the time showed shortly after my arrival. She slowed the video again.

"Both people are gone." I looked at Malone.

"They are." Malone nodded. "The camera isn't placed to catch anything other than the back, so we don't know where they might have gone."

"What about the next day when I was there with Officer Hostas?"

"I can show you that section, but there's nothing at all on it." Joanne pointed at the screen. "The occasional seagull, but nothing else."

"Is there any way to tell if the videos have been altered?" I asked.

The technician answered before Malone could stop her. "We've considered the possibility, but there's nothing I can find to make me think these have been edited. However, we'll send them off to the state crime lab where they have more sophisticated equipment."

"Thank you, Joanne." Malone sounded as disappointed as I felt. "If you find anything when you review the rest, let me know."

"Yes, sir," she answered.

Malone led the way back to his office.

"Have a seat." He pulled a folding chair from behind the door and placed it in front of his desk.

"So pretty much a bust." I sat down across from him.

"Nothing that helps us at all." He shifted some files on his desk. "And I sent an officer to speak with Mr. Zellwen about where he was the day of the murder."

"What did he find out?"

"Zellwen has an alibi. He was in a class that morning in LA."

"I suppose you'll verify his story."

"In the process of doing that right now."

A uniformed officer appeared at the door, and Malone motioned him in. "This may be my confirmation. What do you have?"

"The instructor confirmed that Mr. Zellwen was in attendance at the anger management class from eight o'clock until eleven o'clock the morning of the murder," the spit-and-polish officer stated.

"Thank you, Salinas." Malone nodded. "Would you check with the DMV on traffic conditions for that time period? We should be able to get an estimate of travel times."

"Will do." The officer ducked out.

"Seriously?" I couldn't hold it in any longer. "He was at anger management class?"

"I know. The irony isn't lost on me." Malone leaned back in his chair, arms crossed, his rugged face thoughtful.

"Where does this leave us?" I asked.

"I think you mean, where does this leave me?" His steely blue gaze shifted to mine.

"Sure." I'd really thought the neighbor showed promise. "No word from Cash?"

Malone stared at me. "Caro, leave it alone. I asked you here to review the video. I let you know about Zellwen because you thought he might be the one following you. But the rest, leave it to me. Somehow you've got yourself right in the middle of this."

"Not true."

"Why is it then that I hear from you at least once a day regarding my murder investigation?"

"Because people tell me things." I was offended. I really hadn't interfered. I'd tried to mind my own business. "What do you want me to do? Keep the information to myself?"

"All I'm saying is stay away from the house. Stay away from the neighborhood. Leave the detecting to me."

He acted like I was Betty Foxx, nice but slightly addled, offering advice to him about his murder investigation. Nothing could be further from the truth. I didn't want to be involved. But I wanted Jake's killer found. And I was sure that killer was not Cash.

"Of course." I stood and left before I said something I'd regret.

I could hear his sigh all the way out in the hallway.

BACK IN MY CAR, I gathered the frayed ends of my composure and checked the list I'd made while at the office.

This was a day I had planned for follow-ups. I had no new appointments, but I needed to check back on several clients I'd seen throughout the week and assess how they were doing.

The afternoon flew by. I stopped by to check on Spencer and Cork and was thrilled at the how well they were doing. Cork was getting enough exercise and had stopped getting into mischief. Most of the time. I'd done some research into Irish Setters as library dogs and left some notes with Spencer with information about the program as well as whom to contact. It might not be the answer for them, but I thought it was a possibility, and at the very least it would get Spencer thinking about things they could do together.

My appointment with Nick and Bonnie Humphries and their beagle, Rosie, also went well. The howling hadn't stopped completely, but it was under control.

I looked in on Davia and Nano. The Chihuahua was much less depressed, and Davia had been working with her, getting the little dog out more. Davia was distant with me, not the friendly rapport we'd had before. I suspected Geoff had planted seeds of doubt. Or maybe even told her something that put me in a bad light. We parted without her scheduling another follow-up.

My temper simmered on low, and I promised myself I would not let Geoffrey push me to the boiling point. He needed to be dealt with, but I needed a clear head to figure out how to drive the rat back to Texas.

Audra and Nina were next, and what a success story. They had made so much progress, they didn't need my services any longer which is the end result I'm always after. I confirmed with Audra that Geoffrey hadn't stopped by on his own. She hadn't heard from him, so that was a relief.

I was wrapping up my final visit of the day and was ready to head home when my phone rang.

"This is Caro."

"Ms. Lamont, it's Callum MacAvoy. Please don't hang up." The words came out in a whoosh; I don't believe the man took a breath.

I didn't respond. But I didn't hang up.

I could hear him let out a big sigh. "Caro, uhm, Ms. Lamont, I owe you an apology for the last time we talked."

"I'm listening."

"I was out of line." He sounded contrite. "I had no business bringing your family into the conversation."

"That's right."

"Chalk it up to my enthusiasm." I could almost see him fidgeting.

I waited for him to continue.

"Sometimes when I'm investigating, my zeal gets the best of me and I do or say things I shouldn't. I am truly sorry."

Well, I could surely relate. I often found myself in situations where my mouth got away from me.

"Apology accepted." I would probably regret this. "On one condition."

"What condition?"

"You leave all of my family out of things, you hear?"

"Agreed."

"Okay, then. I think we understand each other." I couldn't believe I was letting him off the hook so easily. "So now tell me why you're really calling me."

"I truly am sorry, but also I need to talk to you. In person. It's about Jake Wylie's murder."

"Then you should talk to Detective Malone, not me."

"Not gonna happen. As you might have guessed, the detective and I aren't on very good terms."

"Not my problem, Mr. MacAvoy."

"Seriously, Ms. Lamont. I have to talk to you."

"Mr. MacAvoy, I'm very busy." I'd accepted his apology, but I still didn't trust him.

"You're tough." He sighed. "Would it help if I said I had a dog?"

"Do you have a dog?"

"No."

"Then no, it wouldn't help." I wasn't sure why I was still listening to the guy. "Get to the point, Mr. MacAvoy."

"I really need your help." His voice dropped so low I could barely hear him. "I've uncovered some vital information."

"All right. What do you know?" I could hear Detective Malone's sigh echoing in my head.

"Not on the phone." He was almost at a whisper now. "Can you meet me this evening?"

You know what they say about curiosity and the cat, right?

"Fine. Where?"

I STRUGGLED A teensy bit with not calling Detective Malone and sharing that Callum MacAvoy had called me. But I didn't really have anything to share, and to tell you the truth, my ego was still stinging from his lecture.

I didn't know how long my conversation with MacAvoy would take, so I ran home and took Dogbert out for a quick walk around the block.

Then with Mama Kat's always-look-presentable admonitions running on auto-loop in my head, I changed into fresh jeans, a cream-colored handkerchief-linen shirt, and my new favorite sandals from Giuseppe Zanotti. I liked his style, part footwear, part jewelry.

Freshening up and changing from my doggie-fur-covered clothes also helped me adjust my attitude. There was nothing wrong with meeting Mr. TV and hearing him out. If after I talked to him, he truly did have some information relevant to the case, I'd call Malone.

We met at Mango Duck, MacAvoy's pick. It was a nice little local bar with an outdoor café. I still didn't see why we needed to meet in person. Surely whatever it was he needed to tell me or ask me could be said on the phone. But Mr. TV had been adamant.

It took me a few minutes to spot MacAvoy when I opened the gate to the outdoor café.

Seated near a grouping of greenery and lush hibiscus plants, he almost blended in with the surroundings. He was slouched in his chair, forest-green *News 5* polo neatly tucked in at the waist of his blue jeans, long legs stretched out under the table. His prime-time handsome face was intent as he scowled at the screen of his phone and tapped a silver pen on his ever-present notebook.

I sat down in the high-backed wicker chair opposite him.

I knew we'd cleared Zellwen, or at least according to Laguna Beach PD findings his alibi had checked out, and I hadn't seen the black SUV again, but I was still a little on edge. I'd had the feeling all the way to the restaurant that I was being followed. If Zellwen had really been at anger management class and hadn't been following me, it didn't change my unease. Someone had been following me.

I shifted in my seat and looked around the patio. I didn't recognize anyone. No familiar faces.

"Would you like something to drink?" MacAvoy offered and motioned the waitress over. There was a Guinness on the table that was already half gone.

"Sweet tea, please, hon." I smiled at the girl. I turned back to him. "So what's the big secret?"

He waited until the waitress was out of earshot. "Here's the deal." He leaned in. "I've done some research on the background of both Jake Wylie and Graham Cash."

The waitress came back with my tea, and he stopped and waited until she'd gone.

"I have uncovered something about Graham Cash and who he really is, but I can't confirm it."

"What can't you confirm?"

He hesitated. His eyes met mine.

Sheesh. Why call me up and get me here if he wasn't going to tell me what it was he needed to confirm. "Listen, MacAvoy, you need to tell me what you found out. Or I'm leaving right now."

Suddenly there was a loud crash of glass, and MacAvoy shot to his feet. A nearby tray of barware had tipped and slid to the floor.

A short, slight man in a trench coat and a 1980s Indiana Jones fedora fell out from behind the shrubs and hibiscus trees where he must have been hiding. He stumbled into the chair MacAvoy had just vacated and then ran smack into our table, knocking over the reporter's Guinness and my iced tea.

Everyone in the café stopped, sandwiches and glasses mid-air. The hostess, as well as a slew of wait staff, came rushing over. MacAvoy had avoided damage by his quick reaction, but I was drenched in Irish beer and sweet tea.

The little trench-coat man righted himself. He looked like he was about to make a run for it.

I grabbed him around the neck.

His hat fell to the ground and left his tousled silver hair exposed.

Wait just a cotton-pickin' minute; it wasn't a man!

"Betty?" I turned her around to face me.

"Let go of me." In her effort at an undercover disguise, her usually colorful eyebrows were two slashes of stark black. It gave her a sinister look. In a cartoon villain sort of way.

I dropped my hold. "What in the Sam Hill are you doing here?"

"Obviously"—she brushed at her trench coat and straightened the collar—"I'm trying to help you and Detective Malone solve this case."

"How much did you hear?" MacAvoy asked.

"Not much cuz you kept whispering." She looked up at him and patted her pocket.

His eyes followed the movement. "Hand over the tape recorder," he demanded.

"What?" The little lady attempted an innocent look. Difficult with those eyebrows.

"That's what you were trying to retrieve from the plant when you knocked over the tray of glasses, wasn't it?" MacAvoy pressed.

She stuck her chin out.

"Give it up."

She reluctantly reached in the pocket of her trench coat and pulled out a small recording device. MacAvoy held out his hand. Betty placed it in his open palm.

MacAvoy popped out a small tape, pocketed it, and handed the device back to her.

"It's state of the art." She slipped it back in her pocket.

"No, it's not. There's a lot better technology out there today." He reached down and picked up the pen he'd had earlier. Betty's stumble through the hibiscus had knocked it to the floor. He looked it over carefully.

"How would you know?" I asked.

He kept his head down not meeting my gaze.

"Is that a recording device?" I asked.

"Lemme see that." Betty leaned in for a better look.

"It's voice activated." MacAvoy gave me a sheepish look.

I guess that answered my question.

"That's really a recorder?" The senior sleuth gave a low whistle. "How does it work?"

"It has a strong microphone so you don't have to be very close." He tucked it away in his pocket. "And you can simply set it on the table instead of having to hide it in a plant."

"Where do I get me one of them?"

"Great. You were both recording the conversation without my permission," I interrupted. "Now, if you two are done comparing nifty spy gadgets, I think we should probably apologize to the staff and let everyone get back to their dinner."

Mr. Prime Time Investigates and Inspector Gadget Grandma Edition suddenly realized everyone in the café was still staring, and those who were close enough were listening in on the conversation.

"Let's go." MacAvoy threw a few bills on the table and turned to go.

Betty tightened the belt on her trench coat and followed.

I brought up the rear, squishing my way between the tables.

Chapter Nineteen

WE STEPPED OUT onto the sidewalk, and my feet slid sideways in my wet sandals. So much for fashion before function. Callum MacAvoy held my arm to steady me as I slipped them off.

If I'd had an ounce of humor left in me, I would have laughed at the spectacle we presented. The tall, clean-cut, heart-throb newsman escorting one soggy, bare-footed redhead, and one trench-coated elderly mini-sleuth who was still clutching her straw handbag and looking like the "before" picture in a cosmetics company's dos and don'ts for older women.

There was a park bench several stores down, and I pointed at it. We needed to regroup. I wasn't sure what was next, but I was leaning toward sending Betty on her way and calling Malone to deal with Mr. TV and his research.

Our rag-tag troop of three had started down the walk when suddenly a shiny, black Lincoln Navigator came by. The big SUV pulled up to the curb and into an empty parking spot. The driver's door swung open and out climbed Geoffrey Carlisle.

In a flash, I suddenly knew who'd been following me, and it wasn't Jake and Cash's neighbor, or a carful of British spies. It was my ex-husband.

He had made me feel unsafe, caused me to waste police time, and to what end? Because he saw a short-cut to a career change?

Geoff came around the car and opened the passenger side door. Davia Sinclair looked like she'd been poured into her Kim Kardashian black-lace pencil dress. He held her arm as she got out, and she took a moment to balance on her strappy six-inch, high-rent heels before tucking a silver Tom Ford clutch under her arm. Then she reached into the Navigator for her final accessory.

Nano.

The little dog was decked out in a matching lace dress and a red tutu.

Now I've got nothing against people dressing up their dogs, and the outfit was frankly adorable. But, this was one majorly unhappy dog. We'd made such progress on Nano's depression, and it was clear Davia and Geoff were in danger of losing all the ground we'd gained.

Davia whipped out a matching red bow and attempted to situate it on Nano's head. The pup looked up at her with small sad eyes, and my heart broke. Geoffrey reached over Davia's lace-clad shoulder to help with the bow.

I turned away to follow MacAvoy and Betty who stood waiting on me. I shook my head.

None of my business, right? Davia had decided not to continue our work with Nano and, from the looks of things, had found herself a new pet therapist.

I heard a low growl and looked back just as Nano nipped at Geoffrey's hand. In a swift move he plucked her out of Davia's arms and tossed her into the SUV. The red bow flew through the air and landed at my feet.

I took it as a sign.

Without a moment's hesitation I marched back to where they stood and latched onto Geoffrey's wrist, twisting his arm like they'd shown us in self-defense class.

"*Never* throw a dog."

"Ouch." Geoff's face contorted in surprised pain.

"Never. Ever. Throw. A dog." I twisted his arm with each word to make sure he understood.

Then I let go and turned to Davia.

"And you." I poked a finger at her. "I don't give a flying fig if you don't want me to work with Nano anymore. That's fine. But get yourself a pet therapist who knows what he's doing. Not this poor excuse for a human being." I pointed toward Geoff who was rubbing his arm.

Davia, eyes wide, backed up and nearly fell off her Manolo Blahniks. "Geoffrey Carlisle." I looked at Geoff, and he backed up, too, like I might hurt him again. "I am warning you for the last time. Stay away from me. Stay away from my clients." I took a step closer with each sentence until we were nose to nose.

"I think—" he began in a placating tone.

"I don't care what you think." I cut him off in my best and loudest you-can't-handle-the-truth tone. "If I ever hear even the slightest rumor of harm you have caused to some animal because of your ignorance and your enormous ego, you'll be sorry, mister. You will be very sorry."

He didn't say anything, but the slight lift of his brow and the derisive smile told me he got a little thrill from making me lose control.

I pushed through the crowd that had collected and put some distance between me and the scene I'd just caused.

Two blocks away, I heard huffing and puffing at my back and realized Betty had followed me.

"Hold up, Carmelita." Her thin arms pumped, and her trench coat flapped as she hurried to catch up. "You rocked!"

I let out a laugh that was part embarrassment and part surprise. "I rocked?"

"Yeah, you told him what for. Don't—mess—with—our—dogs!" She punctuated each word with a punch. "Who was that guy?"

"My ex-husband," I admitted, slowing my pace so Betty could keep up.

We walked a little farther.

"Your ex-husband, huh? My Tommy and me, we were happy." Betty looked wistful. "Marriage is a good thing. But you shouldn't stay married to a nut job."

I suddenly realized I knew very little about her. "How long has your husband been gone?"

"Ten years." She looked up at me, smudged black brows over sharp grey eyes. "Tommy and me packed in a lot of fun before he went. Don't feel sorry for me, Carol."

"Okay, Bertha." I grinned at her.

Pounding feet approached, and we both turned. Callum MacAvoy had finally torn himself from the excitement and caught up with us.

"You sure know how to cause a stir." He fell into step with us.

"Is it safe to go back for my car?" I looked down the street. It appeared the crowd had dispersed.

"If you mean have your ex and his date gone?" He gave me a pointed look. "Then, yes."

"Not what I meant." I hadn't missed the reference to Geoffrey, but I wasn't taking the bait.

"Betty, where's your car?" I wanted to hear what MacAvoy had been about to tell me before at the café but, as fond as I was of the little lady, I was not going to let Betty play detective and put herself in danger.

"It's around the corner from my man Mac's car." She pointed at Mr. TV. "I was following him and when he pulled in by the Duck place, I couldn't find a close parking spot."

My eyes met MacAvoy's over her head. That explained how Betty knew where we were meeting.

Betty crossed over to the other side of the sidewalk and placed her hand in the crook of MacAvoy's arm. "You can walk me to my car, Handsome. I wanted to ask you if that place where you got your pen recorder has any of those electronic tracking thingies?"

MacAvoy looked confused. "Why do you want one?"

"So, I can put it in Carol's car and keep track of her," she explained matter-of-factly.

The reporter opened his mouth and then closed it.

"Listen, hon. I'm sure Mr. MacAvoy can check into the possibility for you later, but right now I'm concerned about Raider. I'll bet he needs to go out, so let's get you on your way."

Betty looked torn.

"You don't need to follow me. I'll tell you exactly where I'm going. I'm going home."

She was a good dog mama. She chose Raider. I knew she would.

Mr. TV and I walked Betty to her car and sent her on her way. My car wasn't far from where Betty's had been.

"Do you want to talk about it?" MacAvoy fell into step with me.

"No." Definitely not with him.

"Okay, fair enough." He backed off without a fuss.

"So why did you want to meet me?" I stopped in front of my car.

"Like I said before Nancy Drew there fell out of the hibiscus tree, I've done some research on both Jake Wylie and Graham Cash."

"Go on." I leaned against the Benz.

"Jake's story is pretty straightforward. California college kid with a knack for computers. However I've come across something interesting with Cash, but I can't get anyone to confirm it. The police won't talk to me at all about the case. The TV station is pressuring me, but that's just the way things work these days."

"What is it you've discovered?" Now I was curious.

"Listen, Caro, I know you don't like me very much, and I think I understand why. Sort of." He smiled sheepishly. "But I'm a good reporter. I check my facts."

"Go on."

"Did Cash ever mention his English roots?"

"No, I think he still has family in the UK, but I don't think he has much to do with them."

"My background research shows no mention of a Graham Cash until the young man appeared full grown here in California." He flipped to a page in his notebook.

"That's interesting. I'm sure you should talk to Detective Malone about this."

"However, there is a member of the royal family whose basic stats match with Graham Cash's. Birthdate, university, etc."

"What part of the royal family?"

"Let's just say, a conveyed title not an inherited one, but a direct connection."

"First, let me be clear that I know nothing about a title, Cash's background, or anything about anything, other than his cat. But if it was true, and Cash had a title but simply wasn't using it, that's no crime. Why do we care?"

"Because if he's being protected because of his relationship to the royal family, that would be a huge story."

"You've mentioned this to Malone?" MacAvoy's far-fetched royal protection theory made my spy theory look plausible by comparison.

"I've left him messages."

"What is it you think I can do?"

"You have access to Cash's home, his office, and the investigation." I turned to go.

"Wait." He stopped me with a hand on my arm. "I'm not asking you to leak information to me, but I can't take this any further without confirmation. The last thing I need is to break a story that's false."

"Sorry, MacAvoy." I walked around my car to get in. "I've promised people who care about me that I'll stay out of this investigation. I've promised Detective Malone that I won't involve myself."

His expression said he wasn't buying it.

"And," I continued, "I've got my hands full with other things as you could see tonight."

To his credit, he held his tongue.

"I can't help you." I got in and started my car. "Good luck with your story."

I drove away, and as I turned the corner I could see MacAvoy walking in the other direction. Maybe he was a good reporter; I didn't know whether he was or not. If he was right and Cash had connections and was getting special treatment, that would be an interesting twist. The problem, however, was he only needed special treatment if he killed his partner, Jake. And I still firmly believed he hadn't.

Bottom line: someone had, and whoever had done it, it seemed very personal. The electric cord around the neck. No distance there. No precision.

And I guess all of those considerations kind of argued against my secret spy theory, didn't they?

Curious enough about Mr. TV's theory to do a little research of my own, when I got home I did a Google search of Graham Cash and the 2Gyz company. MacAvoy was right; there was a slew of information about Jake Wylie, but nothing about Graham Cash except for multiple articles about the success of the company he and Jake had founded.

I'd planned to return Heidi's hair clip to her today and hadn't gotten around to it. I decided I would to do it first thing the next morning. I'd stop by the boutique where she worked, and if the opportunity came up to ask about Cash's family, I would. If they were serious, certainly she would know a bit more about his past.

Whether I'd be reporting what I found out to MacAvoy was something else, but I was intrigued with the idea of a titled geek.

Chapter Twenty

I'D NOT VISITED the boutique where Heidi worked before, at least not that I could remember. It was on the main strip downtown and not too far from Green's Deli, where I'd seen Heidi the other day. It was also, by the way, in the vicinity of Mel's shop, Bow Wow Boutique. As much as I knew Dogbert would enjoy a special treat or toy, I didn't think I'd be stopping in to visit my cousin today.

I'd thought more about how we might come to terms on Grandma Tillie's brooch, but I wasn't quite ready to set up a lunch date to discuss it. A subtle approach would be essential if we were going to have any chance of success at a truce.

I walked into Flirts and was hit with a riot of sound and color. The walls and fixtures were very utilitarian and kept my attention focused on the splashes of pinks, blues, and violets of the beach-inspired ready-to-wear. Music blasted through speakers mounted on top of a cabinet jammed with brightly colored necklaces and bracelets. I didn't see Heidi and wondered if it was her day off. I truly hoped not because I had no other way of contacting her.

A dark-haired girl was folding scarves on a table near the dressing rooms, and I started toward her thinking I'd ask if Heidi was in. Just then Heidi stepped out of the back room, her arms full of hangers. She laid them on the counter and began sorting them.

"Hello, Heidi." I wasn't sure how she would react to seeing me.

"If you've come to apologize, I accept." She glanced up and then tucked a blond lock behind her ear. "You shouldn't have talked to the police about what you overheard."

I waited, silently watching her.

"I should have told the detective about it myself." She continued sorting hangers. "And I shouldn't have barged into your office like I did. I'm sorry about that."

"No, you shouldn't have, but I understand you were upset." I paused. "However, you shouldn't have taken your anger at me out on Betty."

"That's the funny lady with the lipstick eyebrows, right?"

"Yes," I replied.

"I didn't mean to offend her, but those eyebrows are crazy, and she was pretty rude herself." Heidi put a pile of bright-pink plastic hangers into a cart.

"But you're the one who, in your own words, barged in and interrupted." It seemed she needed redirection when it came to apologies.

"You're right,"—she tucked another lock of hair behind her other ear—"and I'm sorry I was rude. I'll apologize. I see her all the time on the sidewalk. She must work or regularly shop somewhere near here."

"She works at my cousin's shop, Bow Wow Boutique. It's a few stores down."

"Oh, yeah. I've seen that store. Puppy nail polish, wedding dresses and tuxes for dogs. Even necklaces and earrings for pets."

"That's the one." I nodded. "Speaking of jewelry, why I really stopped by is to return this." I pulled Heidi's hair clip out of my bag and handed it to her.

"Ohmigosh, thanks." She held it up to the light. "I couldn't think where I'd lost it. Cash bought it for me. It's real gold and pink topaz and very expensive."

"You'd left it on the counter at Baubles. Neeley asked me to return it to you because she was going to be closed for a couple of days."

"I really should be more careful about keeping track of it." She stuck it in her hair. The pink stones winked in the beam of the spotlights over the counter.

"I would have mentioned it to you yesterday, but you left in a bit of a hurry."

"In a big huff, you mean." Some customers had just come in, and she greeted them before continuing. "Really, Caro, the argument between Jake and Cash was nothing. I told the detective that."

"Something else, Heidi. Someone told me Graham Cash is actually a titled Englishman, perhaps even related to the Royal Family." I watched her for a reaction.

"Who told you that?" She fiddled with one of the hangers.

"Had you heard the same thing?" I avoided her question with one of my own.

"I had," she admitted, "but Cash claimed it was just a rumor."

"So you asked him about it?" Was the hint of a title what had made her switch her affections from Jake to Cash?

"Why would anyone want to keep something like that a secret?"

She hadn't really answered my question and wouldn't look at me.

"I don't know." I waited for her to say more, but she just continued fidgeting. "If the police are going to figure out who killed Jake, they need to know everything. If there's anything else, Heidi, please don't keep it to yourself."

"There isn't anything else." She responded a little too quickly.

"What about the fact you were at the house the day Jake was killed and you've never mentioned that detail?"

Heidi went very still and looked up at me, her wide turquoise eyes unblinking for a couple of seconds. "How do you know that?"

I was suddenly glad I'd decided to test this theory in a public place.

"The pink canned energy drink you carry around all the time. It was on the patio, and it was cold. I've never seen either of the guys drink that particular brand."

Heidi pushed aside the hangers and came around the counter. She took my arm and led me to the front of the store where we weren't within earshot of anyone else.

"Listen, Caro." She stopped just short of the big plate-glass window. "I was there, but Jake was very much alive when I left."

"Had Cash already been there?"

"No, I'd been swimming by myself. Jake came outside, and we talked. I took my stuff and I left. I swear, that's all."

"You didn't share any of this with Detective Malone, did you?"

"No. I didn't."

"You need to call him."

"Or what? You will?"

"Yes, I will." I stared her down.

"For Pete's sake, lady, leave the murder investigating to the police!" She spun away and stomped back to the register.

Malone would agree with her sentiment.

Another customer came in, and I took the opportunity to slip out. I stopped and reached in my bag for my sunglasses, and when I looked up, a white convertible was parallel parking a couple of spaces down.

The driver got out and reached in the pocket of his slacks, perhaps hunting for change for the meter, and then he turned and looked straight at me.

Light-blue eyes, blond tousled hair, reddish skin tone. It was the man from the secret room.

"Hey, stop," I called. "I need to talk to you."

He ran back around his car and jumped in, and then shot his car out

132

into traffic without looking. There was a blast of horns from a truck as he cut it off. He had to slam on his brakes to avoid hitting a motorcycle stopped in front of him.

I dashed forward, and this time I got the license plate number. I pulled out my phone and noted it so I wouldn't forget the numbers and letters—CA plates 7DZG461.

The driver of the motorcycle he'd narrowly missed shook his fist and yelled something I was glad I was too far away to hear.

I turned quickly toward where I'd parked and ran right into a man knocking his shopping bags out of his hands.

"Oh, I am so sorry." I helped him gather up his belongings. "I didn't see you."

"You should watch where you're going."

All right, I'd apologized. Sheesh. I glanced up. I knew that voice. It was Wayne.

As I handed him the bags, I noted they were from Mel's shop. "Bow Wow Boutique? So this must mean you're getting the dog."

"Yes, I get my basset hound in two days." His face brightened, and he smiled for the first time since I'd met him. "I got him some special food and some toys to play with."

I couldn't help myself. "Just remember to walk him." I settled the final bag on his beefy wrist. "You know where the dog park is, right?"

"I don't like dog parks." He frowned. "But I'll walk him like I said I would. I filled out all the papers, but that guy at the ARL said I had to wait two days."

"That's not very long." I smiled encouragement. "You'll have Cheeky before you know it."

"Yeah."

"You let me know if there's anything I can do, okay."

"Okay." Wayne ambled on down the sidewalk to his van, and I turned in the other direction toward where I'd parked my car. As I walked I dialed Malone. He picked up right away.

"I have a license number for you." I filled him in on seeing the intruder and recognizing both him and his car. I read off the number from my phone, and he said he would get someone to check it out right away.

"Oh, and one more thing. I just got through talking with Heidi Sussman, and she was at the house the day Jake was killed. She claims Jake was fine when she left, and I think she's probably telling the truth, but maybe the timeline can help you."

"I'll talk to her." His voice was serious as a heart attack. "And, Caro, please . . ."

"I know. Leave the investigating to you."

Like I said, Malone and Heidi were in agreement on that.

I STOPPED BY HOME for lunch where the company was better. Or at least most of those present had no opinion about what I should or should not be doing.

My cell phone rang. Not Mama Kat's ring. I glanced at the number. Not one I recognized.

I answered, "This is Caro."

"Caro, listen. I'm terribly sorry to be a bother, but I can't raise Jake." Graham Cash didn't sound as frantic as when he had called before. In fact, he sounded relatively calm. The reception was clear; I could hear him like he was right next door. I hoped he was as close as he sounded.

Wait a minute. "What did you say?"

"Jake. Like I said, I hate to bother you, but I rang him up yesterday and again today but couldn't reach him," he continued. "Does he happen to be in the office?"

"Cash—" I hesitated. How could he not know?

My mind flooded with thoughts. He had to know. Even if he were out of town it had been on the news. And I knew Malone had tried to call him. Why call me? Why not Malone? Why not his girlfriend, Heidi?

"Is there a problem?"

"It's about Jake."

"Yes, right. Is he there?"

"Cash, Jake is dead."

There was absolute and total silence for a few minutes.

"What?" he choked out. If the guy was acting, he deserved an Academy Award for his performance. "What happened? A car accident? I can't believe . . ." His voice trailed off.

"No, at the house," I said quietly. "You need to call homicide detective, Judd Malone."

"Homicide?" There was silence, and I could hear him take a deep breath and mutter an oath. "What happened?"

"The police have been trying to reach you." I tried not to sound accusatory.

"I've been where there isn't any cell-phone service."

"Where is that, Cash?"

There was a pause. "I can't say."

"Wherever you are you must call Detective Malone at the Laguna Beach Police Department." I gave him Malone's cell-phone number.

"I shouldn't even be calling at all, but I wanted to check on things with Toria. I called Jake. I never thought . . ."

"Can you think of anyone who'd want to kill Jake?"

"Jake? Not a one." There was some background noise. "Caro, I've got to go."

"When did you last see him?"

"He was alive and well when I left the house. Said he'd pick up Toria from you. Wait. Wait. If he didn't pick up kitty, where is she? Is she okay?"

"I've got her and she's doing fine. But, Cash, you really have to call Detective Malone."

"Thanks for taking care of Toria."

"Call Malone."

"I'll try, Caro. I really will."

The phone went dead. I sat staring at it for a while wondering what on earth Graham Cash had gotten himself into.

I dialed Malone and waited for him to pick up. He wasn't going to like this one bit.

Chapter Twenty-One

I SAT IN MY LIVING room surrounded by my dog and the three cats. I'd put on some soft jazz thinking it might relax me. It seemed to be working on the animals. Thelma and Louise were draped across the back of the couch. Thelma casually rested her paw on my shoulder, and Louise had decided my hair was a cat toy. Toria had claimed my lap, and Dogbert had tucked himself against my side. One of the crew was quietly snoring, and I suspected Dog.

I smiled to myself thinking maybe I was becoming more and more like my friend Diana. I have to be honest; I didn't see the similarities as a bad thing.

I'd poured myself a glass of pinot, but had forgotten to drink it. My mind was like a pinball machine. Thoughts about all the events of the past few days and what they might mean bouncing off each other. I couldn't seem to turn it off.

I'd set my cell phone within reach. I didn't expect Cash would call again, but you never know. Sam was up north at a business meeting and had hinted of bringing me a surprise. With Sam, a surprise could be the perfect cup of coffee, or the perfect emerald earrings. You just never knew. He had the unique talent of choosing exactly what I would've picked myself. Regardless of whether it was a thing or an experience, I could use a "good" surprise to wipe out all the bad ones I'd encountered lately.

I patted Dogbert and shifted Toria on my lap so I could scratch her head.

I had repeated my phone conversation with Graham Cash to Malone. I could tell he was still skeptical about Cash's involvement, but I had hopes Cash would call him and we'd finally be able to fill in some big gaps of information.

It felt like I had pieces of the puzzle, but they didn't fit together.

There was the hostile neighbor and his anger issues. The videos with only shadowy figures.

How did someone walk into a house in a quiet neighborhood and murder a guy and then walk right back out and no one noticed?

Then the lawsuit involving the dog app. I'm sure it made Jake and Cash a ton of money, but they'd created lots of other apps. WoofWalker was just one of many. Why in this case would they steal another web developer's idea? Or why would someone think they had?

And the secret room full of computers, the intruder, and then the bare shelves.

Not to mention, Cash's girlfriend Heidi. Her lack of interest in what had happened to the man who was supposedly someone she cared about. And what was the deal with the information she'd been holding back from the police.

Pieces. But how did they fit together?

My doorbell rang. I had to untangle myself from my blanket of pets in order to get up. I turned the music down and went to the door.

"Who is it?" Though I now knew the SUV that had been following me had just been my ex, it didn't change the fact that a killer was still on the loose.

"Malone," came the short reply.

I got a glimpse of myself in the entryway mirror. Not my best look. Cat-styled hair, scattered tufts of fur on the front of my dark-teal silk T-shirt, and makeup that had disappeared hours ago. Mama's be-aware-and-be-prepared admonition flashed through my mind.

Sorry, Mama, I've let you down.

I opened the door.

"Ms. Lamont."

"Detective, please come in."

He followed me to the living room.

"Please have a seat. Can I get you something? Coffee, tea, coke?" I asked. I'd let my mama down in the fashion department, but I wasn't so far gone I'd forgotten my upbringing in the hostess sector.

Malone's mouth quirked in an almost smile. "No, thanks."

He seated himself on the couch.

"So, what's up?" I perched on the arm of the easy chair.

"I spoke with Heidi Sussman, and she confirmed what you'd told me about being at the house the day of the murder." He shifted on the couch, and Thelma stretched and gave him a sidelong glance. How dare he disturb her?

"I'm glad she didn't deny it." I hadn't been sure she wouldn't.

"How did you know she'd been there?" His sharp blue eyes held mine.

"The energy drink on the patio. The day Jake was killed, when I was waiting for you to talk to me, I accidently knocked it over. It spilled, and when I mopped it up I noticed it was cold. It was a warm sunny day so it couldn't have been outside long. She always has this one particular brand with her. I'd never seen the guys drink it, only her."

"Good observations, Detective Lamont."

I took the good-natured dig as an attempt at a peace offering. "Maybe, but not worth much if it doesn't help you."

"Here's another strange development." He rubbed his chin. "I just got the info on the license plate you gave me earlier today, and the car is registered to Heidi's brother."

"Wait, so it was Heidi's brother who was inside the secret room?"

"She never mentioned a brother?" It was a question, but his expression told me he already knew the answer.

"Never." I shook my head. I couldn't remember her mentioning any family, but she hadn't stopped by the office on a regular basis, and when she did, she didn't stay long.

"There's more." Malone leaned forward, propping his elbows on his knees, which garnered another disgusted look from Thelma.

"I'm all ears."

"Heidi's brother's name is Brody Patton." He waited for the significance to sink in.

It took me a few minutes to remember where I'd heard the name, but I finally did. "Which means not only is Brody the intruder I saw pop out of the secret room, he's also the guy who is suing Jake and Cash for a portion of their WoofWalker."

"That's right."

"Different fathers?" None of us would have made the connection because of the different last names.

"Strangely, the same birth parents, but separated by divorce, and the mother remarried. Heidi took the new dad's name. Thus, Heidi Sussman."

"So I'm guessing you see Brody Patton as a suspect."

"Right now, I see him as my number-one suspect." He wiped a hand across his face, the stress of the past week apparent in his fatigue.

Here I'd been thinking I'd had a lousy few days, but they probably didn't even touch the kind of days Detective Malone had been having lately.

"I just came from his condo and he's not there, but we'll pick him up."

"Then what?"

"We'll bring him in for questioning. You might have to come down to the police station and identify him. I may bring Heidi Sussman in as well."

"Sounds like she might have been withholding information to protect her brother." Which would explain quite a bit of her odd behavior.

"Could be."

"No problem. Let me know when you need me and I'll be there."

"Great." He stood. "Just wanted to give you a heads up."

"I appreciate that."

He opened the door to leave and tapped the dead bolt. "Make sure you lock up."

"I will."

I locked up as Malone had ordered. I would have anyway. Then I pulled on my softest T-shirt and flannel pajama bottoms. Mama's distinct ring tone summoned me from the bathroom where I was getting ready for bed.

"Hi, Mama." I patted my face with a towel. "How are you?"

"I'm fine, Carolina." Uh-oh. She sounded serious. "The question is how are you?"

"I'm okay. Why do you ask?"

"Well, I heard from Barbara, who heard from Melinda, that Geoffrey Carlisle is there in California. He stopped by to see Melinda at her little shop and told her you threatened him in front of a whole crowd of people."

"I did." Aunt Barbara, aka Mel's mama, had got that one right.

"Good."

"What?" I couldn't believe what I'd heard.

"I said, good. That low-life has no business coming out there and interfering in your life. I hope you told him to get out of town."

"I can't believe he'd be dumb enough to go talk to Melinda." Was the man stupid as well as arrogant? Or had he gone to Melinda hoping word would get back to me? Probably the latter.

I pictured Mama Kat pacing as she talked. "I know you two girls have had your differences, but you know, bless her heart, Melinda would stand up for you."

"I know she would, Mama."

We talked a little bit more about her big summer barbecue plans, and at one point she offered to make a trip to Laguna if I needed reinforcements. I told her I thought I could handle things with Geoffrey just fine.

After we hung up, I went to the safe where I'd had the brooch locked up and got it out. Warm feelings about Grandma Tillie washed over me.

Matilda "Tillie" Montgomery had been quite a lady, and I had good memories of long summer days spent at the ranch. Mel and I used to play in Grandma Tillie's jewelry, trying on various pieces, pretending to be British royalty. Or Egyptian princesses. Or Mary Kay ladies. We had some fun times.

Then we'd ditch the baubles for outdoor play, chasing around with the dogs, climbing trees, riding horses until we were grimy and dead dog-tired. Then we'd head back to the house where Grandma Tillie always had a big pitcher of lemonade ready as if somehow she'd known the timing.

I opened the musical jewelry box on my dresser and the delicate sounds of *The Yellow Rose of Texas* began to play. I'd had the music box since I was thirteen. A gift from Mel because I was a teenager before she was and she was worried I was going all "girly" on her.

We were driving our families crazy with our fight over Grandma Tillie's brooch. We were denying ourselves the shared memories that were a big part of what made us the proud and prickly Texas roses we were.

It was time to figure this out. I placed the brooch inside the old jewelry box and added "Call Melinda" to my list for the next day. (It might take me a few days, or maybe even weeks, to cross that task off my list, but at least by putting it on the list I was committing to doing it.)

"Dogbert, Toria," I called my two snugglers and headed to bed for the best sleep I'd had in days.

AS I PULLED OUT of my garage the next morning and paused to hit the garage door closer, I noticed my next-door neighbor's car. Apparently she was home from her Alaskan cruise. I'll admit I was reassured to think someone was close by, though I didn't think the diminutive Freda Bauer would be much help fighting off a killer. Still she could call 911, right?

Maybe I was just being paranoid.

Maybe not.

There was still a killer out there, and the police seemed no closer to finding out who had murdered Jake.

I dressed for the day in white jeans and a bright coral top by Maranda, one of the California designers I loved. I had only one appointment. A client with whom I'd been working for a couple of months. Lonnie's mixed breed, Turk, had been having problems since she'd lost her other dog. Animals grieve just like we do, and Turk was lost without Coco, his longtime companion. As a result he'd been depressed and not eating.

After finishing up with Lonnie and Turk, I stopped by the Koffee Klatch to grab a latte before heading to the office.

Verdi was at the desk. A bit of normal in my life was a good thing.

"I'm sorry. If I'd known you were going to be here I would have brought you something."

"That's okay. I brought my own." She held up her own Koffee Klatch cup. "I thought I'd better have plenty of caffeine in case we were in for another parade of people."

I laughed. "You may need more than caffeine."

"Anything new on the murder?" She glanced toward the closed door of Jake and Cash's office.

I brought her up to speed on the events of yesterday, the call from Cash, and what Malone had shared in his visit last night.

My phone rang. I now dreaded those numbers I didn't recognize. Where prior to Jake's murder a call usually meant a new client, lately that sure hadn't been the case.

"Hello, this is Caro."

"Caro, it's Heidi," she whispered. "I'm scared."

"Of what, Heidi?" I pressed the phone against my ear trying to hear her. "Are you okay?"

"Come, please. It might be nothing, but I'm really scared." She hiccupped. "My address is forty-five-fifty Blue Bell, Apartment two B. Hurry." The call abruptly disconnected.

I grabbed my keys. "Verdi, call Malone. I'm going to Heidi's apartment. Here's the address." I scribbled it down and ran to my car.

This time of day, the traffic can be bad on PCH so I took back streets to get to Heidi's apartment. It was a small walk-up, and I climbed two flights of outside stairs as fast as I could.

As I made the turn at the top toward 2B, I felt a terrible sense of dread. I could see the brightly painted yellow door was partly open.

"Heidi?" I called. I touched the bottom with my foot, carefully pushing it slightly open and prayed that Malone was on his way. The door opened a little more, and I tried to peer inside.

"Heidi?" I called again, louder this time. "Hon, are you in there?"

With a wail of sirens, a Laguna Beach blue and white skidded to a stop in front of the building.

"Thank God." I stood aside.

Malone's silver Camaro pulled up right behind the police car.

The officers rushed past me, kicked the door fully open, and went in guns drawn.

They were back outside by the time Malone had reached the top of the stairs.

"Nothing," one of the uniformed officers reported. "The place has been torn up, but there's no one there."

"The young lady?" Malone asked.

The officer shook his head. "She's gone."

Chapter Twenty-Two

I SAT ON THE STEPS and related my story to Malone while the two uniformed officers went door to door asking neighbors if they'd heard anything.

"She said she was afraid," I repeated. "If she was afraid, why didn't she call 911, or call you directly? She had your number."

"I don't know."

"What if she's dead?" I looked up at Malone. "What if I could have saved her if I'd gotten here sooner?"

"We don't know that she's dead." He turned to talk to the two officers who had returned. It sounded like the problem was that no one was home in the other apartments and very few in the surrounding homes. Most people were at work this time of day.

"Let's get crime scene in here." Malone punched some numbers into his cell. "Rope off this area." He gestured toward the stairs and apartment.

"I'll have someone drive you home." Malone reached a hand down to help me up.

"I'm okay to drive." I was shaky, but I could drive.

"Are you sure?"

I nodded.

"We haven't picked up Brody yet, but we're still watching his place, and he has to come home sometime."

"This has to have something to do with him, doesn't it?"

"Let's just say I have a lot of questions for him."

I should have gotten more information from her. I couldn't get past the idea that I'd talked to her on the phone just minutes ago and now she was gone.

I CANCELED MY appointments for the rest of the day and went home. Freda from next door stopped over with a gift from Alaska, a little bottle of Alaskan Birch Syrup, to thank me for watering her plants while she was gone. She'd also caught up on her Laguna Beach news and had lots of questions for me about the murder.

I understood her curiosity, but I was so upset by Heidi's disappearance that I didn't think I was up to re-telling all the details. I gave her a brief overview of the day I'd found Jake and that Cash had gone missing.

Freda politely moved to other topics, and we talked about her trip and other things. She inquired about April Mae, my neighbor on the other side, and when she was expected back. It was soothing to talk about "normal" things for a while. I'd almost forgotten what normal felt like. An hour had passed before I realized it.

My doorbell interrupted us, and not wanting any surprises, I peered out the window. Detective Malone's car was parked in my driveway.

I opened the door and invited him in.

"Ms. Lamont." He stepped inside.

"This is my neighbor, Mrs. Bauer." Freda had followed me to the door. "She just returned from Alaska."

"Nice to meet you." He nodded.

"Nice to meet you, detective. I'll be on my way." Freda slipped around Malone. "Thanks again for taking care of my plants while I was gone. I'll be happy to return the favor if you ever need it."

As soon as Freda left, Malone got right to the point.

"We picked up Brody, Heidi's brother, an hour ago." The detective had been busy. "He admitted to being in the house the day you were there."

"Did he say why?'

"It has to do with the lawsuit. He took a hard drive with the source code for the WoofWalker app. He claims whatever it was he took can help him prove he had a hand in the development."

"So that's why he killed Jake?" I tried to put it together in my head. "I'd think Jake would be more valuable alive."

"I can't tie Brody to Jake's murder yet, but I can hold him on the breaking and entering." Malone paced. "So he's locked up at least until he can make bail on that charge."

"What about Heidi?" I asked.

"He says he knows nothing about Heidi's disappearance."

"Does he know who she might be afraid of?"

Malone shook his head.

I had a sick feeling in the pit of my stomach. I felt a little safer knowing Brody was behind bars for the time being. But the truth was he hadn't seemed all that menacing when he'd been in the house. If you want to talk about menacing, my money had been on Zellwen. But he'd come up with an air-tight alibi.

"Caro, until we figure out what's happened to Heidi Sussman, I need you to stay as far from anyone involved in this investigation as you possibly can. Do you understand?"

I nodded.

"Go about your business as usual. If anyone calls you—Cash, Heidi, that annoying reporter—anyone wanting to talk about the case, call me immediately."

"I will." I was perfectly willing to stay away from anyone involved. You weren't going to find me driving by Jake and Cash's house again and drawing the ire of Mr. Anger Management. I hoped Cash's next phone call would be to Malone and not me. And Heidi, well, I hoped someone heard from her.

"And, anytime you're home." He jiggled the doorknob. "Lock up."

"Got it."

Chapter Twenty-Three

I LOCKED UP LIKE Malone recommended. I have to tell you, Heidi's disappearance had really shaken me. Like Jake's murder, broad daylight and yet no one had seen anything.

I felt terrible I'd been too late to keep Heidi from being kidnapped, and I felt helpless that there was nothing I could do to at this point to help find her. In truth, there was really nothing I could do to help figure out who had killed Jake or to find out where Cash was. I could only take care of Toria and hope Cash would come back soon and help sort everything out now that he knew about Jake.

I couldn't bear to be doing nothing. I looked at my list. No more clients for the day. I'd crossed off almost every item. Almost. There were two tasks left undone. One was to call my cousin, Melinda. This sure as heck was not the day for making that phone call. I needed a clear head and calm emotions. However, I didn't look forward to the other task either.

Don Furry from the ARL had called me and asked for a favor. It seems Cheeky, the basset hound that Wayne (Mr. Cutting Hedge) had planned to adopt, had belatedly been claimed by his owners.

It is really unusual for that to happen after a dog or cat has been at the shelter long enough to be available for adoption, but the couple who owned him had left him in the care of a family member, who had let him get out and then had not been able to find him. The nephew had looked around the neighborhood but hadn't thought to contact City Animal Control or the Laguna Beach Animal Shelter.

Wayne would be very disappointed, but I was sure we could find another dog for him. He hadn't been interested in the Labrador that Chelley had talked to him about because he had had his heart set on a basset hound. I knew there was a basset hound rescue group in San Diego. Maybe if I got in in touch with them, we could see if we could find a good match for Wayne through them.

Don had asked if I would be willing to let the poor guy know. He couldn't leave because they were short-handed and had tried to call but didn't want to just leave Wayne a message with the news. Don feared Wayne might not take it well, and I had to agree, especially after what he'd told me about losing his wife. It was probably best to deliver the news in person. Maybe, if he gave me an opening, I might be able to slip in some grief-counseling information.

I called and talked to the basset hound rescue group and jotted down some information about their process. It sounded like it might be a good solution to help Wayne get a dog that would be what he was looking for, and maybe knowing this wasn't a dead end would help him handle the bad news.

I grabbed my cell phone and my bag and tucked the note where I'd written the info about the San Diego rescue group in my purse.

Just as I was about to leave, my phone rang.

It was Detective Malone.

"Caro, I need your help." I guess we were back to first names.

"Wait a minute. Can you repeat that?" I smiled. I wasn't letting him off the hook that easy. "There seems to be something wrong with my phone. I thought I heard you say you needed my help."

"Point taken." I could picture his tightened jaw. "Listen, I've heard from Cash."

"Oh, thank God." I couldn't quite explain my relief, but I truly felt Cash making contact was good news. Now, there would at least be some answers.

"He says he and Jake had some files they kept on their office computer about threats they'd received."

"Threats?"

"Apparently they received threats on a regular basis, but didn't take them seriously."

"That should help figure out if Jake's murderer is someone who had something against them, right? Like Brody Patton?"

"Graham Cash is on his way back to Laguna Beach and will go through them in person with us, but in the meantime with Heidi missing, he said we should go ahead and take a look."

"Great. Maybe something there will lead you to Heidi."

"Yeah, except Cash was paranoid about the password to the computer. Wouldn't give it to me over the phone. Said it was an extremely simple encryption letter-number replacement formula. The love of his life and then her name spelled out in numbers. He said if we needed help to call you."

"How long did you try before you called me?"

"Not long."

I'd bet longer than they should have.

"We used H-E-I-D-I 8-5-9-4-9 and it was a no go. We've tried Sussman with the same formula and we still can't get in." I could hear the frustration in his voice.

"You're using the wrong starting place." I smiled, knowing what Cash had used. "The love of his life is spelled T-O-R-I-A."

"The cat?" I could hear him mutter the letters.

"Yes."

"Try T-O-R-I-A," he called to whoever was there with him. There was a pause. "And then, 20-15-18-9-1." I figured it was probably Joann, the technician who'd reviewed the videos with me.

"Got it." I could hear a female voice answer. "We're in."

"Thanks, Caro." Malone's relief was evident.

You're wel—" But I was talking to air; he was gone.

"You're welcome," I said to the disconnected phone.

Hell's bells! This was an exciting development. They were so close. Cash had made contact. They had access to new information that could help.

"I knew your daddy wasn't a killer," I told Toria who'd come to see what the excitement was about. Or, if you really want to know the truth, she could have come to see if I was baking more cat treats.

I still didn't know where Cash had been, but I had every confidence now that he was in touch with Malone the whole hot mess would be sorted out. And soon.

My stomach lurched. I only hoped whatever Malone and crew found on Cash's computer, or whatever information he could help them with, would be in time to save Heidi from the same fate as Jake.

I reached down to stroke Toria's soft fur. "You'll be going home soon," I told her. She leaned in and purred as if she knew what I'd said.

"We can't do anything," I told her. "We just have to be patient and wait."

Toria gave a sharp meow that said she didn't like the idea of waiting any better than I did.

Surely Malone would at least do me the courtesy of letting me know if they were able to find Heidi.

When they found Heidi, I corrected myself. I wasn't going to consider the possibility they wouldn't.

I remembered how long I'd had to wait on his report about the angry Mr. Zellwen. Okay, fair enough, he had his hands full, but I needed something to keep me from going crazy until I got the information.

I took a deep breath and then exhaled. I still had that bad news to deliver.

I tucked my cell phone in my jeans pocket and grabbed my car keys. Best to get things cleared up with Wayne and the disappointing news about the basset hound. I checked my bag to make sure I had the information on the rescue group I'd jotted down earlier. He'd had his heart set on Cheeky, but I hoped the idea of getting in touch with the SoCal basset hound rescue might soften the blow of the adoption not working out. In any case, in my experience, it's best to get bad news over with right away.

Chapter Twenty-Four

WAYNE'S HOUSE WAS a drab slate blue and surrounded by the stubble of a lawn in need of care. In the back there was a shed that had probably once also been the same shade of blue. It looked like it needed a new roof and coat of paint. An oleander hedge along the back of his lot really needed trimmed back, and I thought about the expression Grandma Tillie had often used about the shoemaker's children going barefoot. I supposed when he got home from working on trimming up other people's hedges, the last thing he wanted to do was work on his own. The yard was fenced, which would be good when he eventually brought home his basset hound. I was sure the rescue group could help him find a good match.

The "Cutting Hedge" van was parked in the drive, so Wayne was apparently home. A part of me had been wishing for a reprieve.

Wayne answered my knock right away. His big body filled the doorway, but I could still see past him into the house. The meager furnishings were plain but serviceable. There was a couch, a recliner that had seen better days, dining-room chair, and a TV tray currently being used as a lamp table. The living room was not exactly clean and neat, but still not terrible for a guy living alone.

He smelled like sweat and nervously shifted from one foot to the other. I wondered if I'd caught him at a bad time. Maybe he'd just gotten home. The television blared from the other room, so maybe I'd interrupted a favorite show.

It didn't appear he was going to invite me in.

Shoot. This was not a conversation I wanted to have standing on his front porch.

"Would it be okay if I came in?" I pointed past him.

"Oh, sorry. Come in. Come in." He moved aside so I could enter. "I wasn't expecting company."

I crossed the room and sat on the couch which was in direct line of sight to the television. A court reality show was on, and Judge Wanda was about to mete out her punishment for a roommate who'd apparently eaten his roomie's birthday cake and drank said birthday boy's beer. Perhaps the verdict was what had Wayne on pins and needles.

"Is this a bad time?" I raised a brow.

"No, no. This is fine." Wayne turned the volume down and sat carefully on the arm of the chair.

This was going to be a hard conversation, and I truly felt sorry for the man. It seemed like he badly wanted a pet, and we had a ton of pets in need of homes. But I knew he'd had his heart set on Cheeky, the basset hound. Maybe he'd be so happy for Cheeky, knowing his owners had come to claim him, that it would temper his disappointment. Best to just spit it out.

"Wayne, I know you've had your heart set on adopting Cheeky, and tomorrow the waiting period would be over." I took a deep breath. "But today Cheeky's owners called, then came in and identified him and picked him up."

"What?" Wayne jumped up. I hadn't even realized the big man could move that fast. "They can't do that after they deserted him."

"They were out of town, and their nephew was supposed to be taking care of him. I guess he got out somehow without his collar on, and the nephew failed to report it, and so they didn't even know he was gone until they got home from their trip."

Wayne paced back and forth.

"That's completely irresponsible. They should have made sure Charlie was taken care of."

"Charlie? You mean, Cheeky right?"

"Oh, yeah. That's what I meant. Cheeky."

"I'm so sorry, Wayne." I stood and approached him. I'd known the poor guy would be disappointed, but I didn't realize he'd take it this badly. He was really agitated. It was good Don hadn't tried to handle this news with a phone call.

"It's not right." His voice got louder. "They shouldn't get him."

I lowered my voice. It's a great de-escalation technique. It often works with dogs and with people.

"I know you're upset," I said quietly. "But I'm sure they'll be more careful in the future. And we're going to check in on them and Cheeky and make sure he's okay."

"He's not okay!" Wayne roared. "This is not okay." He pounded the table.

I felt so bad for the guy. Forgetting his sensitivity to touch, I laid my hand on his forearm in an attempt to calm him, and he immediately shook it off.

In doing so, he flung his arm out and hit the lamp on the TV tray. Broken pieces of the shattered lamp flew. One of the shards embedded itself in Wayne's hand, but he didn't even flinch.

Blood began to drip on his jeans, but he was so agitated, he didn't notice.

Man, I'd known he would be unhappy, but I hadn't thought he would take it this hard. He was so upset he couldn't speak, his face red, his breathing labored.

"Hang on there, buddy." I could see the kitchen through a doorway and figured it would be a good idea to rinse the cut. "You've cut yourself and you're bleeding. Let's take care of that."

He'd stopped yelling and seemed to be in shock. He stood, eyes wide, but he made no move toward the kitchen.

I was beginning to reevaluate whether we'd made a good choice in approving him for a pet adoption. His references had checked out. He didn't have a criminal background. He was new in town, not originally from the area, but Don Furry had done an extensive interview with him. Nothing we'd seen had indicated the kind of extreme instability I was seeing now.

I hurried through to the kitchen and grabbed a handful of paper towels.

"Let me take a look at that cut." I still thought it should be cleaned, but we'd start with trying to stop the bleeding.

He shook his head. "It's nothing." He wrapped his hand with the paper towels I'd brought but still didn't move. "I've cut myself way worse doing yard work."

"Well, this cut is bleeding a lot. Let me get a damp towel and we can at least clean the wound a bit and see what we're dealing with." I went back to the kitchen, tore off some more towels, and ran them under water. As I did, my gaze landed on the glittery hairclip beside the sink. It looked like it had been washed, but it still sparkled like gold.

Real gold and pink topaz and very expensive.

I felt like I'd been sucker punched. Like all of my breath left my body. I'd seen this hair ornament before.

I picked it up and turned.

Wayne stood in the doorway. One look at his face—the rage gone, an emotionless stillness in its place—told me he knew I'd recognized the hair clip.

"It was you."

He nodded slightly.

Holy Blindside, Batman!

"Is Heidi alive?"

"For now she is. Her boyfriend will come for her, and then I'll take care of him."

I stepped away keeping my eyes on him, but I didn't have far to go. My back was against the counter.

"Where are you keeping her?"

He didn't say anything, but his eyes slid to the kitchen window.

I'd noticed the shed earlier near the overgrown hedge. "Is Heidi out there?"

Wayne didn't answer, but his expression confirmed it. He raised his hand to look at the cut, and as he did more blood dripped on the floor.

Great, he was keeping Heidi in a shed out back, he was bleeding all over his floor, no one knew where I was, and I didn't think he was losing enough blood so that I could pin my hopes on him bleeding out.

I tried to remember some of the moves from my self-defense class, but he had the clear advantage in size, and he was blocking my escape route. If I could distract him maybe I could make a run for it.

Reaching behind me, I tried to remember what else had been on the counter. Dirty dishes, a greasy rag, the roll of paper towels. No knives that I could picture.

Suddenly, my phone rang. I looked at Wayne.

"Answer it, but no funny business," he said flatly.

I pulled it from my pocket and glanced at the caller ID. It was Betty. Wonderful. I was about to be killed, and my last phone call would be from a pajama-clad senior citizen.

You've seen those shows where the person is being held at gun/knifepoint but they're able to send a coded message to the person on the other end of the phone signaling they were in danger? All without alerting the killer?

Yeah, that was not going to happen here.

I pushed the button to answer. "Hello, Betty."

"Hey, Carol." Her voice crackled through the phone. "I'm at your house. When are you coming home?"

"Wait. What are you doing at my house?"

"You said I could have those dog-trainer books for Raider, and I had some time today so I stopped by to get them. I got here and your neighbor lady thought I shouldn't be sitting outside in the sun so she let me in. I'm inside. Nice house you've got. Nice dog, too. Your cats are okay. That one is funny looking. Weird ears."

I was so upset that Betty was at my house and had talked her way inside that I almost forgot I was about to be offed.

"Betty, you don't just go into people's homes uninvited."

"I didn't, Carmen. You invited me."

"But I'm not home right now." I suddenly remembered Wayne. "I'm at—" I stopped, noting the crazed look in Wayne's eyes and the vein that pulsed in his forehead. I didn't dare risk it. He could snap at any moment.

Wayne lunged forward and took the phone from me, pushed the disconnect button, and threw it on counter. It immediately rang. Betty didn't like being hung up on.

He pushed the end button again. It rang again. He stomped off, marched through the front door, and threw it outside.

So much for that lifeline. No phoning a friend for me.

It only took a few minutes for him to get to the door and back, but I knew I had to take the opportunity try to escape. Otherwise, my chances for survival did not look good.

Before he could get back to the kitchen, I ran for the back of the house. I wasn't at all sure where I was running, but I figured there had to be a door that led outside or at the very least room with a lock that would buy me some time.

"No, you don't." The man was big, but he was quick. He grabbed my hair and yanked me back. "You sit right here." He dragged me to the living room and pushed me down on the couch. "I gotta figure out what to do about you."

He'd begun to pace again.

"Why?" I asked quietly.

"What?" He stopped and stared at me, beads of sweat stood out on his forehead and upper lip.

"Why, Wayne?" I'd put together (I know, too little too late) that everything had started when Wayne arrived on the scene. That day at the office when he'd claimed car trouble had obviously just been a ploy. He must have been looking for Jake and Cash.

"They ruined my life."

I could see the emotion ran deep, but I somehow didn't see him and the tech billionaires running in the same circles.

"How so?"

"They invented that awful WoofWalker." He let out a short breath and narrowed his eyes.

"How is it awful?" I encouraged him to talk.

"My wife, Lena, bought one."

"Yes?" I needed him to keep talking because I needed time to think.

I wondered if I screamed really loud if there might be neighbors who were close enough to hear. I tried to picture how close the next house was and if I'd seen any cars in the nearby driveways.

"Lena and our dog, Charlie, started walking every day. They both lost weight, and she lost interest in me. Then one day I come home from work." His eyes filled with tears again. "And she'd run off with a guy with a Weimaraner that she'd met at the dog park. Left me and took Charlie."

Ah, his wife hadn't died. She'd left him. And the same with his basset hound. I remembered the way his facial expression had changed when I'd mentioned exercise. The pieces of the puzzle fell into place.

"Jake and Cash didn't cause your wife to leave," I said softly. But in his confused mind, he believed they did.

Maybe I could use elbow-to-the-gut move we'd learned in self-defense class. I was not going down without a fight.

"If they'd never invented WoofWalker, I'd still have Lena and Charlie. Now I've got nothing. They gotta be stopped."

I racked my brain for some way to get away from him and call Malone. If only I'd told someone where I was going.

"Cash calls me." I threw out the idea in desperation.

"Why?" He gave me a hard look, but I had his attention.

"To check on his cat."

He eyed me like he wondered whether to believe me.

"I can call him, but I'll need my phone." Wayne didn't need to know that Cash never answered when I called. Or that he called me from some unknown number that I couldn't call back. I needed my phone. My only tie to the outside world. I only hoped it was still in working order.

"Fine." He started toward the door, but then stopped and came back toward me. "But I've gotta make sure you don't make a run for it again." He ripped the electrical cord from the broken lamp.

"Move." He pointed at the dining room chair.

I reluctantly moved to the straight wooden chair. Wayne wrapped the cord tight around my hands and then around the arms of the chair.

My stomach tightened with fear. The vivid picture of Jake as I pulled him from the pool flashed into my mind. I pushed it away. I gave myself a mental shake. Get a grip. Don't panic. Keep a clear head.

Once he was sure I wasn't going anywhere, Wayne disappeared outside and in short order was back with my cell phone in his bear-like hand.

He loosened the cord from my wrists and handed me the phone. "Call him."

It was risky, but I had to try something. I weighed my options. Maybe I could pretend to call Cash but call Malone instead. But how would he know where to come, unless I could somehow give the address?

I hesitated. If I gave my location, I knew I'd be dead before help arrived. Probably Heidi too. There had to be a way.

"Dial the number," Wayne instructed. "Then hand me the phone."

So much for my calling the police idea.

I called Cash's cell number and handed the phone to Wayne.

I could hear his recorded voice mail greeting. Which was what I'd gotten the times I had tried to contact him since he'd been missing. Wayne listened, and his face got redder.

"Listen, you scumbag. I've got your catsitter and your girlfriend," Wayne yelled. "You better get here fast. Call me back on this number."

He slammed the phone down on the coffee table, and it immediately rang.

Wayne reached for it and answered. "Hello." He listened. "Wrong number." He put it back down on the table.

It immediately rang again.

I couldn't see the screen, but I was more than certain it was the persistent little pajama-wearing senior citizen calling from my house.

Wayne grabbed the phone up and reared back to throw it at the wall.

"He can't call back if you break it," I said quietly.

He hesitated and dropped his arm.

"It's probably another client." Of course, it was Betty. "I'm afraid, whoever it is, they'll just keep calling."

"Make it stop." He held his hands over his ears.

"Hand me the phone."

He did and I glanced at the screen. Shoot, just as I thought, it was Betty. I made a big show of muting the sound. But I also hit answer, leaving the line open, and then laid the phone on the TV tray praying Wayne wouldn't notice.

"See the ringer is turned down. You don't need to throw it again.

I'm sure Cash will call back right away and you won't need to kill me." I only hoped Betty was listening and would call Malone.

"Wayne, tell me about your dog. He was a basset hound?" I could see now why it had been so important to Wayne to adopt Cheeky.

He nodded. "Charlie."

Ah, that explained the earlier slip of the tongue.

"We got him right after we got married. I loved that dog." He wiped his eyes.

Quite the sentimental guy for a killer.

If I could keep him talking maybe he wouldn't realize he hadn't retied my hands. And maybe Betty would figure out I was in trouble.

"And your wife, Lena. Have you tried to contact her? Maybe she'd let you share custody of Charlie." The longer I could keep him calm and talking, the better my chances were. And Heidi's.

He grunted. "I don't think so. I tried and tried to talk to her, and she got one of those no-contact things." His shoulders drooped. "So now I can't even visit Charlie."

I thought that was probably a very good idea, but I kept those views to myself.

"Tell me about Charlie. Did you get him as a puppy?" I had to buy as much time as I could. Or figure out a way to escape in case Betty didn't hear the exchange and call Malone.

Wayne launched into a story about his basset hound as a puppy, and I worked hard to keep him talking, prompting whenever he seemed to be winding down. I glanced around for a weapon or an exit. If Plan A didn't work, I needed a Plan B.

I wondered how much time had passed.

The path to the front door was blocked, and the dash for the back of the house had been unsuccessful before. I spotted a hammer leaning against the wall by the couch. A potential weapon if I could get to it.

"No, you don't." He stopping talking and followed my gaze. "Let's get you tied up again."

Before he could get me secured to the chair with the electrical cord there was a knock on the front door. We both jumped.

"You'd better answer it," I said, watching him closely. "Your van is out front. They will know you're home."

Wayne hesitated. He turned toward the door and then back to me.

The pounding got louder.

"Open this door." Oh good grief. It was Betty. I had so been hoping for Malone.

Still, you take what you can get, right?

I screamed as loud as I could. "Betty, go for help!"

The door, apparently not locked, swung open, and Betty burst in, her usual straw handbag hiked up in the crook of her arm, thin hands waving ready to karate chop the big man.

And Mr. TV must not have been far behind her. As I looked out the open door I could see a *News 5* camera crew setting up on the front yard.

Betty continued to circle the room and make wide swipes with her arms.

Wayne cocked his head. He stood immobile in the middle of the room, awestruck. Eyes wide, mouth open, mesmerized by Betty's crazy dance around him.

Where in the Sam Hill were the police? I prayed Betty had called them.

Wayne came to and advanced toward Betty. The little pajama-clad lady suddenly stopped her wild arm movements. She planted her feet wide apart like she was readying for *The Gunfight at the OK Corral.* Except the lady didn't have a gun.

I stood and moved toward Wayne hoping to get between them. I had to keep him from hurting Betty.

Determination on her face, Betty grabbed the handle of her purse, and with a broad swath swung it at Wayne's head. There was a sickening thud as purse met skull.

Wayne stopped in his tracks and then went down.

Unfortunately Betty was unable stop the momentum of her killer purse swing, and I was in the same flight path.

I felt the impact on the back of my head and then a sharp pain before I crumpled to the floor.

I tried to focus, but there were two Bettys standing over me and suddenly also two Malones.

"What've you got in there?" I asked Betty. "A brick?"

"How'd she know that?" The two Bettys turned and looked at the Malones.

And that's the last I remembered until I came to on a stretcher in the mobile Medic Unit.

Chapter Twenty-Five

THEY THOROUGHLY checked me over at the hospital and then released me. The wound on my head was painful but superficial.

Once he'd verified I was all right, Malone had let me know he had his hands full with Wayne and he'd get my statement the next day.

I had several offers for a ride home, Betty among them, but I opted to wait for Sam who had just gotten back into town. I was grateful to Betty for her part in saving my life, but I didn't think I could take any more Betty-type excitement today.

Sam Gallanos walked into the hospital cubicle, and I felt all the emotion of the past few hours wash over me in a rush.

I bit my lip. I would not cry.

Sam framed my face in his hands and carefully kissed me. "How's your head?"

"A little sore." I poked my fingers through the tangle that was my hair and touched the back of my head where there was a sizeable lump. "But given what could have been, I'm great."

"Caro." His face turned pale, and he bent down and rested his forehead against mine. "I can't even think about what could have been."

I squeezed his hand. "Take me home?"

"Absolutely." He raised his head. "Ready to go?"

"More than ready." I slid off the examination table they'd parked me on and stood, waiting a few minutes to steady myself.

Sam helped me get situated in his car and, though I knew he was full of questions, allowed me the quiet peace of the short drive to my house.

My car was parked in the driveway. Malone must have arranged for someone to drop it off. I was glad. I didn't think I'd be ready to revisit Wayne's house any time soon.

"Oh, no." I reached for my bag. "I don't have my keys."

Sam reached in his jacket pocket and held them out. "I ran into Detective Malone in the lobby." He smiled. "Wayne Kemper's injuries had to be checked out too."

"Oh, yeah." I started to shake my head, but then realized that was going to hurt. "Wayne took the brunt of Betty's brick-filled purse."

"If you don't mind, I'd like to come in," Sam said as he helped me out of the car and up the steps.

"If my disheveled state doesn't frighten you, sugar, come on in."

He settled me on the couch and brought me some water so I could take the pain pills the ER doc had insisted I might need later. He was right. This was later, and I needed them.

"I understand Heidi was found?" Sam asked.

"Yes. She was okay. He had her tied up in his shed." I shivered to think what a close call we'd both had.

I swallowed the pills and handed the water glass back to Sam.

"I'm still a little confused about Betty Foxx's part in what happened." He sat down on the arm of the couch.

"It's complicated." I rubbed my temple and carefully dragged a hand through my hair. "Betty had called me repeatedly while I was at Wayne's house, but I couldn't risk an overt call for help because Wayne wouldn't have hesitated to kill me."

Sam flinched, but said nothing.

"So when Wayne handed me my phone to turn down the sound, I muted the ringer to keep Wayne calm. But I also hit the button to answer Betty's call and left the line open, hoping and praying that she'd hear what was going on and call the police."

"Brilliant. And she figured it out."

"She made out enough to know I was in trouble but didn't know where I was. Luckily, my crazy daily to-do list saved the day. I'd left it on the counter, and I'd listed talking to Wayne about the basset hound."

"Thank God."

"Betty called Malone from my house but then drove to Wayne's house herself. She had the address because they'd had some things from Mel's Bow Wow Boutique delivered to him."

"Unbelievable." Sam shook his head.

My doorbell peeled and I started to get up, but the pain pills were beginning to work their magic. I felt like my limbs weighed at least eighty pounds apiece.

"Stay right there." Sam motioned. "I'll get it."

He went to the door, and I heard low voices.

Graham Cash hurried into my living room. All that had happened since I'd last seen him flashed through my mind. Again, the emotions of the day got away from me, and I felt the quick sting of tears behind my eyes. I leaned back and took in a deep breath and let it out, attempting to compose myself.

"Bloody happy to see you're all right, Caro." Cash crouched down in front of me. "Are you all right?" He took my hands in his.

Toria, across the room snuggled up with Thelma and Louise, raised her head, her ears perked up. She knew that voice.

"I'm fine." I waved away his concern. "Really. Perfectly fine."

The green-eyed tabby's eyes were round and bright as she jumped down from her perch and trotted to Cash, meowing a greeting.

"I think someone missed you." I grinned.

He leaned over to pet Toria, but continued to eye me. "I cannot begin to tell you how dreadfully sorry I am to have put you in the middle of this horrid situation."

"You've talked to Malone?" I asked.

"I have. He and I were going through the files Jake and I had saved of what we felt were credible threats, when he got the call from the woman, Mrs. Foxx."

Cash picked up Toria and hauled her inside his leather jacket cradling her against him. "I hope you haven't caused any trouble." He touched her nose with his finger and smiled. She purred in response.

"No trouble at all." I reached out and touched her soft grey fur. "In fact, I'll miss her."

Cash dropped his head. "I had no idea when I left town on business that the short time I'd asked you to keep Toria would turn out to be so long."

I waited for him to continue, hoping for more information.

He looked up and pinched the bridge of his nose. "Jake had said he would pick her up from you. He was the only one who knew my unexpected travel plans and that I'd be out of reach for a while."

Again, I didn't say anything waiting for him to explain.

"On business," he added.

"I won't ask what kind of business." I slanted a look at him. "Because my guess is you can't say."

"It's not that I don't trust you, Caro." His eyes met mine. "Good grief, after this who wouldn't? Thanks to you Heidi is alive."

"I'm glad she's safe." I kept my tone neutral because in my mind Heidi still had some explaining to do. "It was a close call. I think you may have some ground to make up with your girlfriend."

Cash gave a crooked grin. "I feel terrible about what she went through, but the truth is she's not my girlfriend. We had broken things off the day before I left town. I'd figured out she was unnaturally interested in this dispute and pending lawsuit regarding our dog exercise app."

I was glad to know he'd been on to her. "I guess you now know Brody is her brother. And the one suing you regarding Woofwalker."

"Yeah. The bloody thing has caused so much grief that I may not fight him. At this point it might be best to be shed of it."

"I can understand your feelings, but it's your work. Yours and Jake's."

"I know I'm probably just talking like a nutter because I feel so gutted over this mess. I feel like I've been pretty naïve about people and their motives." He stood and set Toria on the floor. "Heidi had got this crazy idea in her head that I was related to the British Royal Family. She fancied herself with a title, I guess. I'm afraid I'm disappointingly common."

"Really?" I smiled and shifted on the couch so I could see him better. "You won't believe this, but at one point I got the crazy idea in *my* head, that you were British Secret Intelligence."

I watched his face for a reaction.

His expression went completely blank for a minute, then he bent over and ran his hands down Toria's back. "That is crazy, isn't it? A goofy techie like me." A broad grin split his face as he straightened. "Too much watching MI6 shows on the telly, perhaps?"

His sharp blue eyes met mine.

"I'm sure that's it." I smiled.

"What am I thinking?" Cash slapped his forehead. "I'm beyond sorry to keep you talking. With all you've been through, you need to rest." He took my hand and gave a slight bow. "I wanted to stop by and collect Toria and give you my very inadequate, but sincerest, apologies."

"It worked out." I tried to hold back a yawn. "We can talk more later."

Sam had been silent through the whole exchange. He went through to the kitchen and helped Cash gather Toria's things and then walked him to the door. I could hear them talking quietly, but not what they were saying. By the time Sam came back inside, I had almost nodded off. Between the events of the day catching up with me and the pain pills taking effect, I felt drained of the ability to move.

Sam helped me get a pillow situated so I wasn't lying directly on the lump on my head.

"Thanks." I smiled at him. "That. What Cash said." I tried to enunciate, but I knew my words were slurring. "That was a bunch of hooey."

Sam laughed. "I am sure you're right."

"Darn tootin'." I couldn't hold back my yawn this time.

"Caro, *brisu mou*, get some rest." He tucked the blanket around me.

My cell phone trilled Mama Kat's ring, and I heard Sam pick it up.

I could only hear his side of the conversation, but it was enough for me to know there was going to be a very long interrogation, aka phone conversation, with the Queen of Guilt in my future.

"No, I'm sorry, Caro's not available. She's asleep," he said politely. There was a pause.

"Who am I? I'm her friend, Sam Gallanos. Yes, it's a pleasure to meet you, too, Mrs. Lamont. Ah, Katherine, of course." Another pause, much longer. "No, I've been to Texas but you're right, I have never been to an authentic Texas barbecue." He laughed. "Certainly, Katherine. I'll tell Caro you called."

Holy Guacamole! I was done for.

I laid my head back down on the pillow carefully. I knew it had been a mistake not to call her and fill her in, but sometimes, like when you've nearly been killed, you get a pass. You get to be a coward. I needed to sleep first, deal with my mama later. After a good night's rest, I'd rally my courage and call her.

I'm sure Sam locked up when he left, but I was out again before he'd closed the door.

Chapter Twenty-Six

THE NEXT MORNING I carefully shampooed my hair in the shower and let my Irish-Setter-auburn curls air dry. I lightly ran my fingers over the lump. The swelling was down, and my spirits were up. Sam had called to check on me, and Malone had called to say I could stop by the police station at my convenience to give my statement.

I still wasn't sure how Callum MacAvoy had gotten wind of Betty's rescue mission. I knew he monitored the police scanner, but he'd been ahead of all the other news stations. Actually ahead of Malone, so he had to have been either been following me or Betty.

At this point, I wasn't sure it mattered.

I was certain he was going to report a sensationalized version of the events, and there wasn't a thing I could do about it. But considering all the events of the past week, I didn't even hold it against him.

The most important thing was that thanks to Betty's quick thinking and penchant for not minding her own business, Heidi was alive, I was alive, and Wayne Kemper was behind bars.

I flipped on the television as I started the coffee. The *Channel 5 News* meteorologist was finishing up her forecast posing in front of a large overlay of southern California. Orange County weather was going to be exceptionally lovely, cloudless and sunny. And I was exceptionally thankful I was going to be around to enjoy it.

The television screen went to commercial break but not before it flashed a teaser. A PR shot of Jake and Cash from their company website. "And up next, the story of two computer billionaires and a tale of murder and intrigue." The main anchor looked into the camera and smiled. "Don't touch that remote."

"Great. I can hardly wait."

Dogbert came to see what I was talking about.

The commercials were over, and the news was back. "Here we go," I told him.

Mr. TV filled the screen smiling like he'd just won the lottery. Well, I guess he'd gotten his story.

"The whole sensational saga started here," Callum MacAvoy intoned in front of a panoramic picture of Jake and Cash's storybook mansion. "And ended here." There was a video roll of Wayne's dingy blue cottage, police cars with flashing lights angled in front of the house.

"Where this man held two women hostage." On the film Wayne was escorted out in handcuffs. (I didn't really remember that part very well.)

"Two Internet tycoons, a software application to help Fido get fit, and a marriage gone wrong. It cost Jake Wylie his life, and it almost cost these two beautiful women their lives as well."

The screen showed side-by-side color pictures of Heidi on the beach in a pink bikini and me in a one-piece and a sash in the Miss Texas swimsuit competition.

Oh, for cryin' in a bucket! Where had MacAvoy gotten a hold of that photo?

That man. I gritted my teeth. I wished him bad karma.

"And today in a *News Five* exclusive, we have in the studio the woman who was right in the middle of the fray when it all went down. Welcome, Betty Foxx."

The shot widened to an interview set, and MacAvoy slid into a dark-brown, plush swivel chair beside Betty. She'd dressed for her TV appearance in a fancy gold pajama set (I didn't know if this was a Jackie-O one or not), and as a fashion accent, she had a red satin scarf flung around her thin shoulders. Her handy dandy wicker handbag sat square on her lap.

"We arrived on the scene together where Ms. Lamont was tied to a chair and Ms. Sussman was bound and gagged in a shed behind the house." MacAvoy's melodramatic delivery made my skin crawl.

"Tell us what happened next." The reported turned to Betty.

"I knocked on the door, but no one answered." She shook her silver curls.

"And then?" MacAvoy encouraged.

"Then I opened the door, saw the killer standing over Carol, and I jumped him." Betty made chopping motions with her hands.

"Wayne Kemper is a pretty big guy, Mrs. Foxx. Weren't you afraid?" MacAvoy asked.

"Nope. Not me. I smacked him with my purse." The geriatric superhero held her purse aloft with big grin and waved the end of the bright-red scarf that matched her bright-red eyebrows.

Good grief, did no one check the woman before she left the house?

Surely her daughter or someone knew she was going to be on TV. Melinda, really? Couldn't you help the lady out?

The camera moved in for a close-up of Betty, and as it did I noticed the glittering pin holding her scarf in place.

I leaned forward to see it better.

It was an antique brooch. A gold basket of multi-colored fruit. Emeralds, diamonds, rubies. It was very familiar.

It was mine.

While I had been about to be killed by a maniac, the little sticky-fingered imp had taken advantage of being in my house, had found Grandma Tillie's brooch in my jewelry box, and had poached it for my cousin.

I'd been soft, thinking about calling a truce, feeling all sentimental, and all the while my sneaky cousin had been plotting to get the brooch back.

I'd been had.

Fine. That's how you want to play this? Well, then.

Game on, Melinda.

Game on, Betty.

Game on.

The End

Pet Treat Recipes

Toria's Catnip Cookies for Aristo-cats

These are preservative free and contain no artificial coloring. They are Toria-tested, and she guarantees even the most high-class kittens will not find them lacking. Not recommended for people to nibble on . . .

You'll need:

> 1 cup of all-purpose flour
>
> 1/4 cup of whole wheat flour
>
> 2 tablespoons of wheat germ
>
> 2-4 tablespoons of catnip
>
> 1/3 cup of milk
>
> 2 tablespoons of vegetable oil
>
> 1 tablespoon of molasses
>
> 1 egg

Here are the steps: (Toria oversaw the prep work. Even staying below the stairs while the treats were baking to assure the highest of quality.)

> Pre-heat the oven to 350 degrees.
>
> Combine the dry ingredients in a bowl (flour, wheat germ, and catnip).
>
> Add the wet ingredients (egg, milk, vegetable oil, and molasses).
>
> Mix until thoroughly blended and then work the mix into a dough.
>
> Lightly flour your work surface. I use wax paper or parchment paper on my counter top to make cleanup easier.
>
> Remove a portion of the dough and use a rolling pin to flatten the dough until it's about a 1/4 of an inch thick.
>
> Cut the dough using a cookie cutter of your choice. I had a crown-shaped one that seemed to please Toria, but there are many fun choices available.

Place the cut cookies on a very lightly greased cookie sheet.

Bake them for 10-15 minutes, or until they are crisp and lightly browned.

Once they've cooled, I'd recommend putting them in several small freezer bags. It's important to remember since these are preservative free, they can spoil and so should be refrigerated. Also, unless you have several cats or your cat entertains frequently, it's best to divide the treats up and freeze them. Then when you're ready to use the treats you can take a bag from the freezer, let it thaw for several hours, and you're ready for afternoon tea.

Thelma and Louise's Southern Chick N Biscuits

Thelma and Louise didn't care for Toria's Aristo-cat Cookies (a little too high flalutin' for them); instead they prefer these down-home Southern Chick N Biscuit treats. Perfect for a barbecue or a Sunday afternoon lounging at home on the windowsill.

You'll need:

 1-1/2 cups of cooked chicken (shredded)

 1/2 cup of chicken broth

 1 cup of whole-wheat flour

 1/3 cup of cornmeal

 1 tablespoon of catnip

 1 tablespoon of soft margarine

Here are the steps:

 Preheat the oven to 350 F.

 Combine the chicken, broth, and margarine and blend well.

 Add the whole-wheat flour and cornmeal.

 Blend well with a fork.

 Knead the dough into a ball and roll to 1/4 inch.

 Cut into one-inch-sized pieces and place on a cookie sheet.

 Bake at 350 degrees for approximately 20 minutes.

 Let cool and serve.

Easy to make and cat-tested, these treats are also preservative free so you'll definitely want to refrigerate them. (That is, if there are leftovers.)

Acknowledgements

We'd like to thank the amazing team at Bell Bridge Books and especially Deborah Smith, our editor. Your talent and expertise have made our books better books and us better writers. Thank you from the bottom of our hearts. Also, Danielle and Niki, the Marketing Queens at BBB, you rock.

Christine Witthohm, our agent, at BookCents Literary Agency, you continue to awe us with your zeal and support to help us reach our goals.

A huge thank you to the mystery-writing community where we've learned so much and discovered so many new friends.

Also a heartfelt thank you to our readers. You've touched our hearts with your enthusiasm for Caro and Mel. You have become our family. We love to hear from you! Keep those letters and emails coming, and make sure you sign up for updates so you don't miss what we're plotting next.

Mary Lee and Anita aka Sparkle Abbey
SparkleAbbey.com

About the Authors

Sparkle Abbey is the pseudonym of two mystery authors (Mary Lee Woods and Anita Carter). They are friends and neighbors as well as co-writers of the Pampered Pets Mystery Series. The pen name was created by combining the names of their rescue pets—Sparkle (Mary Lee's cat) and Abbey (Anita's dog). They reside in central Iowa, but if they could write anywhere, you would find them on the beach with their laptops and, depending on the time of day, with either an iced tea or a margarita.

Mary Lee

Mary Lee Salsbury Woods is the "Sparkle" half of Sparkle Abbey. She is past-president of Sisters in Crime-Iowa and a member of Mystery Writers of America, Romance Writers of America, Kiss of Death, the RWA Mystery Suspense Chapter, Sisters in Crime National, and the SinC Internet group Guppies.

Prior to publishing the Pampered Pets Mystery Series with Bell Bridge Books, Mary Lee won first place in the Daphne du Maurier contest, sponsored by the Kiss of Death chapter of RWA, and was a finalist in Murder in the Grove's mystery contest, as well as Killer Nashville's Claymore Dagger contest.

Mary Lee is an avid reader and supporter of public libraries. She lives in Central Iowa with her husband, Tim, and Sparkle, the rescue cat namesake of Sparkle Abbey. In her day job, she is the non-techie in the IT Department. Any spare time she spends reading and enjoying her sons and daughters-in-law, and five grandchildren.

Anita

Anita Carter is the "Abbey" half of Sparkle Abbey. She is a member of Mystery Writers of America, Romance Writers of America, Kiss of Death, the RWA Mystery Suspense chapter, and Sisters in Crime.

She grew up reading Trixie Belden, Nancy Drew, and the Margo Mystery series by Jerry B. Jenkins (years before his popular *Left Behind* series). Her family is grateful all the years of "fending for yourself" dinners of spaghetti and frozen pizza have finally paid off, even though they haven't exactly stopped.

In Anita's day job, she works for a staffing company. She also lives in Central Iowa with her husband and four children, son-in-law, grandchild, and two rescue dogs, Chewy and Sophie.